JEWEL SEA

ALSO BY KIM KELLY

Black Diamonds
This Red Earth
The Blue Mile
Paper Daisies
Wild Chicory
Lady Bird & The Fox

'colourful, evocative, energetic' – *Sydney Morning Herald*

'impressive research' – *Daily Telegraph*

'Why can't more people write like this?' – *Canberra Times*

KIM KELLY

JEWEL SEA

Jazz Monkey
Publications

Jewel Sea

EPUB: 9781925786279
POD: 9781925786286

Cover design by Alissa Dinallo
Cover image: Shutterstock montage
Map: Entitled Fremantle to Windham, 'The Nor'-West Run', Blue Ruin Design
Author photograph: Dean Brownlee
Printing: IngramSpark

Publishing services provided by Critical Mass
www.critmassconsulting.com

For another chance.

*What leaf-fring'd legend haunts about thy shape
Of deities or mortals, or of both,
In Tempe or the dales of Arcady?
What men or gods are these? What maidens loth?
What mad pursuit? What struggle to escape?
What pipes and timbrels? What wild ecstasy?*

'Ode on a Grecian Urn', John Keats, 1819

*

*The tide swells, the storm uncurls –
What is love but grit for pearls?*

'Purple Daze', B. Sharpe, 1912

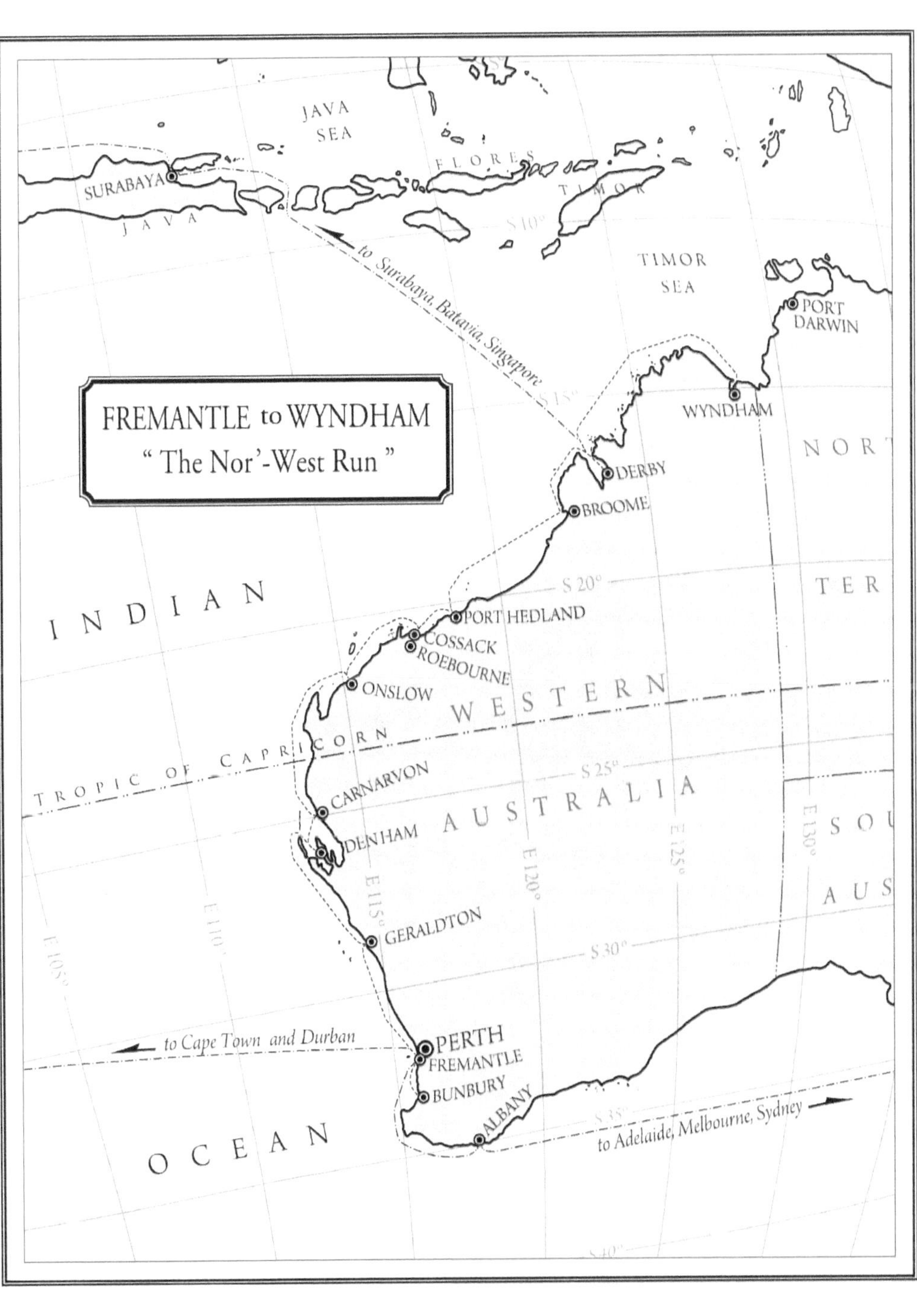

FREMANTLE to WYNDHAM
" The Nor'-West Run "
JAVA SEA
FLORES
TIMOR
SURABAYA
JAVA
S 10°
TIMOR SEA
PORT DARWIN
to Surabaya, Batavia, Singapore
WYNDHAM
S 15°
NOR
DERBY
BROOME
INDIAN
S 20°
TER
PORT HEDLAND
COSSACK
ROEBOURNE
ONSLOW
WESTERN
TROPIC OF CAPRICORN
CARNARVON
S 25°
AUSTRALIA
DENHAM
E 130°
SOU
E 125°
AUS
E 120°
E 115°
E 110°
GERALDTON
S 30°
E 105°
to Cape Town and Durban
PERTH
FREMANTLE
BUNBURY
ALBANY
S 35°
to Adelaide, Melbourne, Sydney
OCEAN
S 40°

STRING

Tyger, tyger, burning bright …

IRENE

The heat rushes in with the opening of the door, breathless, fag-end of summer heat, and yet it's March. Isn't it? My blouse sticks instantly to my skin, and it's only nine o'clock, whatever it is.

'Roberts.' Even my voice seems liquefied somehow, draining across the terrace boards towards the balustrade. 'It is March, yes?'

'Yes, Miss Everley,' he replies, this Roberts, my driver this past fortnight home at Retreat. At all hours he's impossibly erect, smiling, handsome: waiting at the bottom of the steps for me in the full glare of the rising sun now, his jacket is an essay on the insanity of man. I want to peel the deep-green worsted off him. He informs me: 'It's the twelfth – of March.'

'I don't believe it.'

'Do you ever believe anything?' Marg is following me out, keys in one hand, voluminous handbag always in the other. Humidity means nothing to her, unseasonable or otherwise – she was formed in Calcutta, mostly.

I turn on the stair between her and Roberts, and whatever I might have quipped in response leaves me in the click of the door as Marg shuts it behind her. I take in the broad, strong back of my redoubtable companion, my navigator – Marg, Margaret Carson – the twitch of her wrist as she locks the door to save one of the maids forgetting to fasten the snib inside. I look up at the house, our dear Retreat, the place where I was formed, mostly, and an odd hesitation catches me, an unfamiliar whisper of finality. This house, this haven of cool, pale stone, is a place I have yearned to leave ever since I knew how. Despite the solidity of both her dimensions and her market price, there has always been some impermanence beneath my feet here, some sense I have only ever been a visitor. I leave this house for months at a time several times a year. I don't know why I should be even vaguely reluctant to leave her now.

Why I should sense – what? I look out the other way again, beyond Roberts and the car, to the yachts on Freshwater Bay, bobbing and billowing through their breakfast diamonds as they do every sunny day. The Indian Ocean pounds at Cottesloe somewhere behind us, but here at the sheltered mouth of the Swan it's always calm, almost always a swimming day. And I am treading water out beyond the baths: *Irene! Irene! Come back – a shark will take you!* my mother calls me in from some ancient memory. I can see her waving to me, pleading from the shore, calling in to me my one abiding fear, and it's not of sharks but that I'll take a fatal gulp one day if I don't keep moving. I resume my way across the lawn to the car now. Don't stop pedalling, my motor seems to say, but I think I might be losing sight of what I'm pedalling for. In fact, I know I am, but I can't stop for dread, or for dearness. God, Mum, but I still miss you. Is it really seven years?

'Tigs?' Marg is at my ear, whispering the college-days sobriquet she saves for affection and for warning, but mostly for bemusement. 'What's wrong?'

'Just a little bummed,' I whisper back, and there can be no uncertainty about that. I'm always a little bummed, a little hung-over from the night before. Stale. Sticky. God – this heat. I could go for a swim this minute, let myself drift out past Rottnest, all the way to Madagascar.

'Poor thing,' says Marg, with absolutely no sympathy. Why should she have any? It's she who tidies up after me, makes sure I'm out of bed in time to meet my ship, keeps all my secrets in that handbag, too. She is my sturdy veneer of respectability, and she keeps me on the move.

I grunt and slouch into the back seat with my own contempt for myself, and she says, sighing her way in beside me: 'Going to be one of those days, is it?'

One of those bummed-out days when I'm gruntish and rude the whole while? No, it's not. I mutter: 'Just contemplating Derby.'

And I am now. If it's hot here in Perth, it will be land of the damned up in Derby – even if autumn decides to begin somewhere over the next two weeks. I can no more forego Derby, though, or more specifically Everley Station, fifty miles east and ten degrees hotter, than I can my next gin. Old Hal, dear old Dad, would never forgive me if I never came home again there – if I went as far away as I should. Neither would my sisters: Oceanna and Marie will have the children gathering bouquets of lavender lambs' tails for me, the mulla-mulla blooms we gathered when we were small ourselves, so blue against the red desert earth, petals crumbling onto white linen as so many tiny sprinklings of sky. They'll have polished my saddle and plaited Freckle's mane, too. I adore my family. I have three nieces and two nephews who adore me back; I even like their fathers, because they like mine – they both work for him; our family is tied up in such a sweet bow. But, apart from the station's more or less uncanny resemblance to a forgotten corner of hell, there are only so many relentless conversations about the cattle trade one can reasonably survive, dinner chat turning always to the latest best plan for keeping the West Kimberley free of ticks and natives, ladies' lounging always consumed with which of my sisters is pregnant first again and who is due when.

As it is, I spent little more than a week with them all here at Retreat over Christmas, making an excuse that I had to get back to Melbourne, for the hunt with Marksy, to whom I've been notionally, mutually non-engaged for the past five years. I still haven't told Old Hal the real reason for my increasingly frequent trips east over the past couple, can't tell him that my 'shopping' forays entail lunching with the editor of *Australian Life Weekly*, can't even tell him I have a job, for too many reasons to count. Can't tell him Marksy and I will never marry, either, though I'll be quizzed daily for the long, long month I'm home. Marksy Densforth is not at all fond of girls, in that way, and I'm twenty-seven years old – Harold Wellington Everley, beef baron, will work it out eventually, even if the father part of him can't: this heifer will never breed. Not if she can help it.

'Well, it'll be a relief to get out on the deep blue, won't it,' Marg says beside me, as Roberts noses out onto the Esplanade, bound for Fremantle, for our ship. 'Catch some breeze. You know, I do love a lingering summer, but don't you think it's odd that the Doc hasn't come for the past three days?'

'Hm,' I reply. Indeed our Doctor, the relieving evening breeze, hasn't visited for who knows how long, but I'm distracted now by quite another linger. Last night: Stuart. I've left my preventative at his place, round the bay at Mosman Park, my little rubber stopper – left it on the corner of the bath. I'm not likely to need such contraceptive insurance in the next little while but it's annoying. I almost tell Roberts to head down that way so that I might retrieve it, just in case, but Stu won't be there, he'll be in town, and I'm not asking his man for it. I squeeze my temples with too many never-agains. Stuart Wakefield. I've had a sweet spot for him forever, since short pants, my boy up the road, and he's awfully unhappy with Clarice, takes every chance he can to get away from Adelaide to be free of wifey, but I'm never hot-suppering with him again. I am beginning to use men as I use gin: as an excuse to avoid the truth. I can't keep wasting time like this, wasting life, here, going back and forth along the coast, spending more time on ships than in the world. In my life. It's what *Aus Life* expects me to do, scratch out my first-class caricatures for them, to satisfy the insatiable hunger so many Australians have for unwitting self-disgust, but it's not what I must do. Amusing as it is.

A stepping stone, I've promised myself ever since I took on the job, half a joke with Marksy, that's all it is. A stepping stone to London, to Paris, to Prague, to proper living, proper writing. Things to write about. Actual experiences. But I'm holding my stepping stone so close, it's going to sink me one day if I don't let it go. 'Purple Daze', she's my baby, my little monthly column. Mine. How could I let her go?

I close my eyes for a moment and the sun stipples every sense in gold through the peppermint leaves that overhang the road, all thoughts dissolving in the singular desire for a cigarette.

'Bleeding heck!'

Roberts swerves sharply at the corner, skidding the wheels across the gravel verge of the narrow road as another car comes on towards us, too fast for the cliff-top grade. 'Move over!' He punches the horn as the other driver whooshes around us with a wave, and Marg's fingernails dig into my knee. 'Devil's Bend,' Roberts mutters, before turning to apologise. ''Scuse me, Miss Everley, Miss Carson – but I tell you, something should be done about this bend before someone gets killed. Too many cars on the roads these days – and hooligans with 'em.'

Someone will get killed, I have no doubt. But it won't be the fault of the bend, will it. Roberts and just about every other driver takes this corner instead of wending down the bayside Esplanade. There's the problem and the answer: creatures of habit, aren't we all, caught in the illusion that one way might be better than another, quicker, easier, when it would have been more prudent to take the scenic route. I should get off the ship at Broome for Singapore and keep going.

I look down at Marg's hand, still gripping my knee, aware that I didn't so much as blink. I am that heedless, hooligan driver myself. Where am I going? I touch the string of seed pearls at my neck, a slim thread of cool in all this heat, and I don't know. I don't know much but that there is something wrong with me. There must be.

FIN

He looked down onto the street from the hotel window, the place no more familiar to him in this morning light than it had been in the dark, when he'd arrived last night, on the train from Kalgoorlie. Before that, he'd come up from Esperance by the goldfields mail coach; before that, Adelaide, by fishing schooner. Now, Fremantle. There wasn't much to see: another hotel across the way; warehouses; a shipwright's offices. No-one much about but those getting on with their working day. A seaman wheeling a barrow of rope; a post boy on a bicycle.

It was almost ten am – time to go. Last boarding for passengers at eleven. His pulse began to race once more. It was one thing to impersonate a fellow getting about for work, as he had done since slipping out of Sydney, more than a month ago. It was another thing to resume his gentlemanly guise. Merely a suit of clothes. A collar that scraped against his fresh-shaved neck.

Finlay McFarland. That was the name his mother had given him, and perhaps the only real thing about him. He checked himself in the mirror again, a final time.

Seven years it had been since he'd left his naval uniform in a public lavatory in Auckland, left it there with the name he'd been given by the orphanage. He straightened his tie again now, and slipped away again.

'Off to meet the king today, are yer, feller?' the hotelier remarked as Fin returned the key to the room.

'Might be my lucky day, you never know.' Fin winked over the doubts that seethed beneath his skin, no matter which skin he wore. Was the line of his part straight enough, or not messed about enough; sideburns even or clipped too close; shoes shined or scuffed? Who was he today? Yesterday, he was a miner on his way in from the goldfields for a holiday by the sea; and now?

The water jug on the cabinet behind the hotelier had a spout shaped like a swan's head and it stared at Fin, too, curious. 'That'll be four shillings and nine pence,' the hotelier said and then he pressed: 'Where you off to today? On your holidays, didn't you say you were?'

'A holiday of sorts,' Fin replied with a regretful shrug. 'Attending to my brother's affairs in Bunbury. He died last Friday, so I'm meeting with his solicitor.'

'Oh, pardon me, I am sorry to hear of your bereavement,' the hotelier said, embarrassed.

Fin placed a silver crown on the countertop, as if it weren't among his last, and replied absently: 'Don't be sorry. We never got on all that well.' He smiled at the hotelier long enough to set a firm impression. 'I'm not too fussed about Bunbury, either.'

The hotelier smiled weakly, sympathetically: good, this is what the man would tell the police if asked about a traveller matching his description: Scotsman, six feet, two inches tall, fair complexion, hazel eyes, fashionably attired. Well-journeyed suitcase.

'But your change, sir?' the hotelier called after Fin as he turned away to leave.

'Keep it.' Not an amount that might appear ostentatious – just three pennies, just enough to be appreciated, to put a stop to any further exchanges, too. Bunbury? To Fin that was just a name on the map he'd been studying over the past few days.

Out on the street, he resisted the urge to look over his shoulder. In every sense, Fin avoided it as much as possible: to look behind, to see too clearly what trail he'd made, might have caused him to stop, run back to assist those innocents caught in the deceit. He'd been caught himself, in Sydney; didn't realise the fraud played against those ordinary investors until it was too late. *I was just the salesman*, he'd told himself again and again.

But that's not the way the law would see it. Bogus title deeds for fictional properties overlooking the water at Maroubra Beach, deposits of ten percent taken on each – stolen by McElroy & McFarland Pty Ltd, the partnership there in black and white. A haul of £570, a paltry sum, all told, and McElroy had pocketed the lot for himself – hadn't even forked over Fin's portion of the sales commissions. Fred McElroy had stood to make off with well over £4000, if the scam had gone through to its conclusion; but he was in the cells at Darlinghurst awaiting trial now, caught red-handed taking cash. *The thieving bastard. And let those investors have learned a lesson in greed – they should have known it was too good to be true. A parcel of land, with a house built on it, for less than £300 pounds – in Sydney? That's a lesson in stupidity.* That's what Fin told himself now, a weight of irony upon his back. *I am not a thief.*

It's true, he wasn't a thief, not by intention, but he was a fraud. A liar by such necessity it was just about habit for him to deceive.

Where was he heading this time? Malaya perhaps? Or Fiji? Rhodesia? Wherever opportunity took him next – so long as it was out of the country. First, he would get up to Broome, and whatever ship awaited there would decide his next invention. Would it matter where or what? Turn up at whatever shack they'd have there for a customs office and ask for a passport out. It was that easy, bilking customs; he'd done it before, in Brisbane, on the way in to Australia. *My papers, sir? I'm afraid they were stolen, from my room at the pub – back in Wanganui – took my wallet, too ...* And if you arrive at any government office at five minutes to five, you can make a clerk believe and put his stamp to anything.

The warm air sat over the streets like stale breath as Fin continued to Victoria Quay. The glimpses of water that could be seen as he walked were grey, shadowed by the buildings along the foreshore; then a wall of wheat bags two hundred yards long. An ugly, desolate place, he might have thought, if he had never known the cold, or the loneliness of Glasgow. Warmth could never seem stale or uncomfortable in any way to him; warmth was barley soup filling hunger, it was a promise that things could never be too grim. He quickened his step.

He found the ship soon enough, her name, *Koombana*, in black letters on the prow jutting out into the sudden brightness of the sunshine. There was nothing immediately remarkable about this coastal steamer, nothing to suggest, as the *West Australian* shipping news had last night, that the most modern of accommodations awaited within. Whatever was in it, it looked an excellent vessel to Fin. The white rails of her passenger decks, the red stripe of her hull against water made suddenly blue in this burst of light, promised him some kind of liberty. Two weeks on this ship, no policemen, no unexpected strangers, just the sea and a cabin to himself. All along the dock, lumpers and seamen and passengers went about the business of departure, too busy to pay any particular attention to him. A herd of cattle bellowed their way up a ramp and into their stalls amidships on the main deck.

'You've not booked a berth?' the steward said to him as he attempted to board, first class and ticketless.

'Oh? Should I have?' Fin pretended ignorance of the inconvenience he would cause.

'No, sir. Don't worry about it, sir,' the steward was swift to assure the gentleman that he would be accommodated, swift to smooth away any offence, and explain: 'It's just that so many boarding at such short notice makes things difficult sometimes. Catering and all that sort of thing, and the passenger lists are never right. But there will be no problem, sir, never mind. We can arrange your cabin and you can settle up your fare with the purser, Mr Harris, you'll find his window just in here before you come to the saloon doors, forward of —'

'I'll find him.' Fin smiled, stepping past the steward and through the entranceway to first class behind him.

He placed his suitcase against the wall there, but he didn't go on to the purser's window straightaway. He needed a few minutes to collect himself, to decide more precisely who he would be now. He leaned on the double doors of the saloon and exhaled, giving thanks to the sea. *One way or another, you always rescue me.*

MIYA

I am the sea. I am the air. I know all stories.

I see the woman and the man come together and come apart, over and over. Beginning and beginning. Finding each other in the light; drifting asunder in the dark. Always seeking to return to the warmth without which there is nothing at all. The names change, but the story is always the same. I have at least seven myself – names, that is – and only one story to tell.

Only one chance to tell it, too. Only one way to tell it from where I was, from where I lay trapped and waiting, there in the black box. Seven years I had waited, and now I had come so close to the end of my duress, to the end of all constraint, I almost sent my light beyond the edges of the box; I might have lifted the lid with my yearning. But it was not yet time; not quite. Time would come and time would go.

The man with the moustache began to move, closer and closer. I saw him take the money from the bank that morning – £22,500. I saw him walk back towards the ship. I saw him wanting me, reaching across the days until we would meet.

He sent a telegram in reply to the one he had received advising that the meeting must take place on the ship at Port Hedland; they would make the exchange in his cabin. In secret. Given my history, it would have to be arranged this way. Dealing in stolen goods was the highest offence in the trade – worse than murder, the consequence of which could see a man murdered himself.

'Good morning, Mr Davis,' one of the uniformed men greeted him as he took the steps back up to the promenade.

But Mr Davis barely saw him, so foggy was his view. He took his case containing the money to the purser, to the ship's safe. He signed it in.

They knew each other, the purser and Mr Davis, from all his trips between Perth and Melbourne, and Perth and Broome, for his trade. The purser didn't ask what was in the case; that was not for him to know. He asked instead, rhetorically, meaninglessly: 'Back Nor'-West again, sir?'

And Mr Davis said: 'Yes.' And then he said to himself, to me: 'I will return to Broome only for this season, and after that...?' He walked on, back towards the saloon. Alone, in himself. He patted his coat pockets, by habit; and they were empty pockets, although he was so very wealthy. He found his handkerchief in one of those inside the coat and patted the sweat from his brow with it. He was a good man. A heavy-hearted man, coming apart. The woman, Mrs Davis, the one called Cecily, had been so unkind to him, and for so long; such a betrayer. Ruthless. Selfish. The divorce, although necessary and inevitable, had been so very hard for him to bear. The shame of all the details of her adultery in all of the newspapers; the shame he felt at having disappointed his god; at having disappointed himself. I didn't want to use him as I knew I must; he was different from the others. His want of me was for a deeper need, for love. A delusion, at least at first. He thought he might take me to New York. Change everything. Start again. Heal his pain.

Yes, I pitied him, but he had made his choices, as any other man.

He was here, and so was I. He was the one I had been waiting for. It was all unstoppable, unless he changed his mind. I would try my hardest to make sure he didn't.

Soon we would come together, at last. Now, it was time to leave. Now, it was time to return.

IRENE

The sky and the water are one, merged beyond the flat smudge of the cargo yards like a crease made across the middle of a blank sheet of paper – carbon-smeared. I stare at it, listening to the soft whir of the ceiling fans high and discordant against the faint growl rising from below decks, song of another journey almost begun. The ice in my glass clinks as I suck the last of my Tom Collins from a cube.

Marg turns the page of her magazine with an irritated flick and a sigh loaded with admonishment that it's only eleven o'clock. I'm not much interested in her opinion at this moment; I'm only concerned that I feel marginally better than I did before downing this gin.

I turn my head to tell her across the table that she might consider having one herself, with an extra slice of lemon in it, but as I do I spy something interesting step through the saloon doors. Nice suit, tailored by someone with a good eye for the human form. If Marksy were here he'd insist we invite it to dine with us on the strength of the tailoring alone. Generous lapels, too, crisp high collar – an American perhaps? He can't be colonial-made, surely. My hand dives towards my notebook that's slid down between my hip and the arm of the chair.

Just when the passenger list on this voyage was looking diabolically dull, too – same old fishbowl load of Nor'-West nouveau riche and over-inflated public servants. I can't keep telling that joke on these jaunts, can I? But yes, I must: it's an *Aus Life* favourite. No louder laugh than the one we reserve for the matriarchs of this the fattest state displaying their worth by the lengths of their pearl ropes, each plump bead a perfect round of fifty grains in weight and as perfectly, lustrously white; they parade themselves like Russians queens, while their husbands, czars of the red desert, wouldn't be seen dead in anything but their dusty corduroys. My dear Old Hal included – God, but Dad must never, *never* know the things I say in my 'Purple Daze', even if half of it is fiction. He must never discover I'm B. Sharpe, otherwise unknown as, and increasingly notorious with every inch that's published. Increasingly earning the umbrage of the premier, too, Wilson, who told me himself over our holiday cocktails at Retreat, 'If ever I find out who that dreadful fellow in Melbourne is, I'll be giving him a piece of rough, old-fashioned truth.'

Something of a runaway engine these days and it all began here, in this saloon, twenty-five columns ago, on this very ship – this very pretentious little ship, with all its violet moquette upholstery. Such a fuss the Nor'-Westers made of their luxurious *Koombana* when she launched, too, as if she doesn't pull into ports made of nought but tin sheds. How could I not have a laugh at this scene? It has to stop, though. Sometime. Now perhaps. Make this my last story for the paper. Can I? When I'm settled in with the family, in Derby, covered in nieces and nephews and all full of pudding, I'll tell Dad what I really want, what I really mean to say: *Dad, darling, guess what. I'm going off to London. It's time. I must. Please, let me go* ... His eyes will grow round and bleary with sadness. He'll tell me, *Tiger, no – it's too far away.* And I'll have to beg, just as I did going back to Adelaide to finish my degree, after Mum left us. He'll never get over losing her the way we did; neither will I. But staying in the fishbowl will change none of it.

The man in the remarkably nice suit is looking at the bookcases, intently, and I'm scrawling out a quick sketch of him already, such is the slippery tangle of all my equivocation. My word, do we have an intellectual non-colonial here, I wonder, a *reader*? *Inform the captain immediately!* I scribble. *This here is a first-class library we have aboard the SS* Purple Peapod *– one that'll be worth a fortune*

*one day as there's not a cracked spine to be found in it. Quick –
all hands to the decorative bookcases! Protect the tomes from the
enigmatic interloper! In a rush of rattling nacre the non-Nor'-Wester
is thrust out onto the promenade for a game of quoits.*

But when I glance over my shoulder at him again, he's still at the
books. Or is he? He might just as well be looking at himself in the
mullioned glass of the bookcase doors; taking off his hat, running a
hand across his chin, he might merely be assessing whether or not
a shave before lunch might be in order. Just as likely, he might be
surreptitiously looking at the room, assessing the company, perhaps
taking a moment to suppress his astonishment at all the violet
moquette in here, set off as it is to such glaring effect by the emerald
carpets and gold leaf ceiling detail. *Gee whizz*, as they might say in
America – I say it every time I enter this realm myself. One never
tires of the visual assault: it's impossible.

But gee whizz twice, I catch sight now of a smirk in the glass.
Our eyes meet in the reflection, just for a second; the smirk deepens,
and he looks away. Who *is* he?

'Don't you dare order another,' Marg hisses, assuming I'm
looking to catch the eye of a steward.

Couldn't be further removed from that desire, suddenly. The
man in the suit has turned away slightly, returning his attention
to the books, opening the cabinet door, perhaps only looking for
something to read after all. His clipped-close hair is a silvery
blond; his physique is trim, tapering; he slouches on one hip like
Endymion, tall and well sprung. An air of careful nonchalance.
Thirty, perhaps? Thirty-two, I decide. I want him to turn right
around so that I can see the colour of his eyes; his tie; the cast
of his nose now obscured by the panes. I want to see him naked.
Whoever he is, I'll be having him for dinner.

I crunch down on a piece of ice, curl my tongue around the jagged
cool, and I reply to Marg: 'I want that man at our table tonight.'

'Irene.' She frowns out the name saved for outright disapproval.

Her approval is not a consideration, though; never has been.
We've known each other quite a long time, since Fremantle Ladies
College; Marg arrived from India in the middle of Third Form; we
were fifteen. We weren't particularly close at school, being from

different castes as we are. My father looked at hers with suspicion, thinking him a dim-witted soldier, although Major Carson had served in the British Army with some distinction before retiring out here; while Major Carson looked at my father with equal although always polite disdain, believing Dad to be an uncouth, ill-mannered bumpkin, so reckless he allowed his youngest daughter to sit the Adelaide Uni Junior Exams – all true. One is a self-made man of trial and error and hard-won triumph; the other a man made of obedience, of faith in order and protocols – and too accustomed to the cards falling in his favour. Dear Major Carson lost just about everything he owned in the pearl price crash of 1904 and then whatever was left went down with the fleet of luggers he'd invested in – the majority of them smashed to smithereens the following year by a storm off the coast of Wyndham. It was awful for them; us, too: 1905 was the year of all bad things. As I mourned Mum, Marg mourned the loss of her future as it had been promised to her, and we've been together like this ever since. I owe her rather a lot; but she owes me, too.

I tell her again: 'I want that man to dine with us tonight. Find out who he is.'

'You will find yourself in terrible trouble one day,' she replies, but she'll do as I ask, because that's what she's paid to do.

I'm already deciding what time he will meet me in my cabin. And biting the end of my pencil with first-stage regret: *where* is your preventative, Tigs? Damn that decision not to detour up to Stuart's to retrieve the thing when I had the chance. Can hardly pop out to the shops for a replacement: such paraphernalia is not carried under the ladies' counter at Boan Brothers, nor prescribed to the unmarried – damn that I have never managed to acquire a medical admirer, only ever lawyers and money men. This fornicatrix must order by mail then, my 'Veil of Confidence' shipped in from San Francisco – long way to go to enjoy hot suppers however one chooses. The man in the suit chooses two books and turns around, finally. I see his face. God, indeed – or chiselled by the hand of. I'm already deciding I'll probably take the risk. I laugh at myself: he's probably batting for the British Army, like Marksy: that suit really is far too nice. So's the blunt square of that jaw; the shadow flash along that cheek.

'I mean it, Irene. I do worry about you, you know.'

I know she does. Marg is a good stick, through and through, but I know she's worried most about what would happen to her if something unfortunate happened to me. I absolutely intend to sort that out before I move on, by obtaining a husband or other suitable appointment for her. What she lacks in superficial physical and financial allure she makes up for in every other more important way; she deserves to have her future restored.

'Excuse me,' I hear the man in the suit say across the room, on his way through, passing another passenger at the doors. 'Good afternoon.' His accent isn't American. Something else – deep and well enunciated.

Marg tosses her magazine onto the table. 'Nothing but rubbish in that lot these days. I think I'll go and get a book, too – take me away from getting caught up thinking about you any further.'

'Go on, then – be a devil.'

I watch her make her way to the bookcases, smiling her own good afternoon at that other passenger just arrived: it's Mr Davis. Abraham de Vahl Davis, pearl dealer, no doubt making his way back to Broome for the start of the season. Now there's a man who looks distracted. Dear, dear Mr Davis. He couldn't lose a penny if he threw it in the ocean, but he's been through an ordeal all right. Such a refined, gentlemanly gentleman, devoutly religious, too. If it's not bad enough to have your wife cuckold you – both to another man, and to another business, her very own, selling frilly smalls – it's fairly horrible to have the entire nation find out all the lurid details as reported in court. She ran off with a travelling shoe salesman: to South Africa; abandoning two children; and returning four years later to make cosy with the lover in some tatty little boarding house in Sydney. Just awful in every way, even if only a fraction of it is fact. But then who am I to judge? Some people just can't settle, can they?

I wave to try to attract his attention. He's a favourite of mine, for his easy, intelligent conversation; although, perhaps he won't be so jovial this trip. Oh well, I'll endeavour to cheer him up. He's standing in the middle of the saloon like a lost boy, rubbing the steamy humidity from his spectacles with his handkerchief, so it takes a moment for him to see me, here in the only slightly less tepid atmosphere inside. He waves back, but he doesn't smile. In 'Purple Daze' he is generally disguised as Ishmael of the *Peapod*, my wise and wily survivor of the vicissitudes of trade and racialist bigotry, and my lampooner in cahoots – God, can we share a laugh, and we've shared quite a few, all the way to Melbourne on one occasion – though he doesn't know of my secret scribbling, either. He'd be as mortified as Old Hal if he knew the half of what I got up to.

'Miss Everley.' Almost a smile as he nears. 'How lovely to see you.'

'And you.' I hold out my hand to him, and as he touches it with the whisper of a kiss, a lovely thought flits into my mind, an odd one, too: Marg and Mr Davis. A twenty-year age gap, and a vast one of religion to go with it – he's Jewish; she's C of E – but there is something sweet in the idea, something in it for each of them, and I know Marg would do anything for the right man should he ever come along. She'd convert; she'd go Hindu if need be. Something to explore here for me, even if it's only the firming of friendships – that won't do anyone any harm. Perhaps he might employ her in some other capacity, if love is not appropriate – a hostess for his famous parties on Roebuck Bay? I give him my most insistent smile and demand of him: 'You must promise to dine with me every night. I won't get through this without you.'

'Ha.' His chuckle is far too brief and weary, but he accedes. 'Anything for you, my dear. Anything you wish.'

'Is that right?' I tease him. 'Careful.'

FIN

'Your luggage, sir?' the purser, Mr Harris, asked him upon the payment of the fare and the allocation of his cabin.

'Hm?' Fin glanced over at his suitcase, where he'd left it against the wall opposite the saloon doors, as if he might have been expecting it to answer for itself.

'Where will the steward find your trunk, sir?' Mr Harris asked more specifically.

Fin smiled, mildly impatient. 'Nowhere on this ship – I have only the one case with me.'

Mr Harris nodded, but he looked again at this last-moment passenger a little longer than was courteous. 'What is your business in Broome …?' Mr Harris asked him, taking a second look at the particulars he'd just noted down. 'Mr Sinclair?'

Sinclair was a name Fin hadn't used in such a while it crashed out of the purser's window now, almost startling him. James Sinclair: the name that one of the nurses at St Stephen's had chosen for him, after the police had delivered him there, to the orphan home for babies. He had often wondered how the nurses chose the names of all those babies. Did they have a book? Did they name them after sweethearts? All those wee bairns born of whores. He'd certainly never been called Mr Sinclair before. Jimmy. Able Seaman. Toe-rag. Bastard. Shiny Arse. But never Mr. Who was he here? Mr James Sinclair, a name, a past he would bury at sea once and for all, this time. But in this instance he was

20

a gentleman from Melbourne, of 31 Finlay Street, South Yarra – an address he'd just made up.

He raised his eyebrows a fraction, enough to signal to the purser that his business was not for him to know and told him only, with ambiguous disdain: 'Broome? I am called to inspect an investment there.'

He almost said an investment of property but stopped himself. The buying and selling of real estate was something he had recently come to know almost as well as he knew life at sea; he even had a vague idea of the state of the game out here – land values were only just now recovering from a tumble they'd taken around the time he'd arrived in Australia, some financial panic that had been all over the papers then. But he knew little about Broome itself. He turned away before the purser could ask him another question; before he opened his mouth again, he'd find out something of the place, with any luck in the books he'd just plucked from the library: a slim volume entitled *The Letters of Lady Broome*, which promised to detail vice-regal life in this state some thirty years ago, when it was still a colony, and another entitled *Western Australia: The Past and the Future*, a rather thick volume on industry in the region – gold, pearl-shell, beef – which promised a good nap this afternoon if not much useful information.

He continued down the promenade, leaving his suitcase where it was, leaving it to the purser to summon a steward so that it could be brought to his cabin. Number eleven: one of the staterooms on this top deck, starboard, just aft of the stack. It was a single-berth cabin with a window view out to sea, a cabin he could ill afford: he only had a little over £39 left; enough to get him out of the country, but that was it. He'd had to leave in too much of a hurry to take all his money with him; he'd cleaned out the contents of the cashbox at the office the second after he saw the police make off with McElroy, but he'd had to say a swift and bitter goodbye to the £113 he had squirrelled in the bank: his savings for a plot to call his own. He'd had an eye on Narrabeen, in Sydney's far northern reaches, the tramline due to be completed this year; a beach he'd never see again. As he moved through the first-class accommodations entrance way now, his mind cast about for new possibilities, miles ahead. He couldn't seriously contemplate picking up the real estate game wherever he washed up next – that was too much a temptation of fate. Perhaps he'd learn a new trade altogether, reinvent himself as a pearl dealer, on his way back to Britain, disappear into Dutch Java on the way – he'd never been to that part of the East Indies, but he'd heard that even lowly clerks and bookkeepers lived like kings there. Alternatively, he could charm that beautiful woman in the saloon out of a slice of her father's fortune: the way she had looked at him, she looked ripe for it. He could beg a loan from her – no, convince her to invest in some new venture. He was a criminal, whether he'd ever meant to be one or not, so why not drop all hope of respectability and behave as a swindler should?

Because that wasn't who he really was.

Who was he?

James Sinclair. James Sinclair. He drilled the name back into himself as he searched for number eleven. What had the purser said? Something about it being easy to find, the cabin could be approached from this interior corridor or from the cross corridor leading off the promenade, so designed to draw in the breeze. For a moment Fin couldn't see any numbers at all. The line of green carpet he walked upon was patterned down the centre with white flags, each containing a single star. The stars danced before his eyes, as all his names crowded round him. James Sinclair: Glasgow. Jim Smith: Auckland. Jim Finlay: Brisbane. And then for a time, Finlay James, before he dared to call himself by the name he'd longed for, the name that was truly his: Finlay McFarland. He could still see the pages, floating as white sails among the stars. He'd been thirteen then, all half-starved knees and elbows, as Matron Babbage, the house mother of Alloway Boys' Home, would say, and as he'd been a bright and obedient lad, she'd had him taken into her office there to see if he might be bright and obedient enough for clerkly work, sent over to the post office rather than destined for Braefield Industrial with all the other boys. When he'd been asked to put a handful of letters from the doctor into some files, matching up the names, he was less struck by the information on who had bad teeth and ringworm than he was by the realisation that everyone at the home had a file. When Matron was called out on some urgent matter, he found his own, and he read every word. He read his mother's name: Marianne McFarland. *What are you doing there! James Sinclair!* Matron was so furious her stinking spit had sprayed his face. *You wicked boy. You wicked, wicked boy.* And now, the reality sank through him like an anchor: wherever he made land, he'd have to find yet another someone else to be.

For a moment, as he stood there in the corridor, it seemed too much. To have waited so long to be Finlay, to have edged towards this self, himself, so carefully, and now to be no-one again. To be on the slip again. But then he saw the words, those words in the file as routine as bad teeth and ringworm, that had set this fate in train: *DATE OF CONVICTION: March 22, 1880, Prostitution & Vagrancy.* And over the page: *PARTICULARS OF DEATH: Bridewell Prison, November 1880, tuberculosis.* And the scrap of coarse, cheap paper from her that lay between the forms, begging to see him one last time as she was dying, calling for him: *Please, bring my baby Finlay to me. He is innocent, even if I am not.* He would never know her story, her suffering, but the desperation of her love called to him across all time. She had been no illiterate streetwalker: her handwriting was beautiful. It set his feet going again now. He would always be someone – for her.

He found the door of number eleven and turned the key. The cabin was spacious, furnished in oak and brass and that loud bordello purple that was everywhere about this ship. Purple curtains pulled back with thick gold cord, purple quilt on the bed, little purple settee. Extraordinary: such an unremarkable ship from the outside, and so much madness going on inside. So much opulence for so few, there wouldn't have been more than two hundred or so berths in all, first *and* steerage, but she was tricked up like the *Lusitania*. In fact, there *was* no steerage, the little ship was so full of swank it held nothing less than second class. He almost laughed. It was something about Australia that amused him and confused him at the same time: he never quite knew if they were putting it on. Who was laughing at whom? He would miss this country; he thought he'd made a home here. But it wasn't to be. He'd been duped, not merely by McElroy, but by his own need to believe; and it would never happen again. How could he have allowed himself to be played so?

One thought sat in the back of his mind like a crumpled tram ticket: if he gave himself in to the police, put his hands up, did his time – for his part in the fraud, however unwitting it was; for his desertion from the navy, too – it might all be over in a matter months, as long as he could find a decent lawyer to plead his case well enough. Cop the desertion and a heavy fine. Afterwards, he could get on with his life, as who he was meant to be – Finlay. Only he couldn't risk it working out for the worse. How could he convince a decent lawyer to take his case – without a bag of money to pay him with? The desertion might mean as much as a year away in itself, combined with the fraud, and the fraud combined with the desertion might mean as much as five. Five years in prison. Six? He wasn't going to prison, not for a day, not at all.

I'm innocent.

To avoid looking into the small crowd of faces of those who might beg to differ – the investors back in Maroubra, and the mates and the sweethearts he'd slipped out on over all his travels, too, all those he'd ever charmed and as quickly abandoned when it was time to push on – he let his mind be occupied instead with the electric fan on the ceiling of the cabin; it was operated by a switch on the wall. What a novelty; what a marvellous invention: so useful and effective, one day every room in the world would have one, he supposed. Perhaps he'd make a new life selling them – in Siam.

There was a knock at the door; the steward brought in his suitcase. 'Would you like me to unpack for you, sir? Arrange any laundry?' Finlay shook his head, 'No,' and gave the fellow a shilling to go away, gave him a look to see to it that he was not to be disturbed unless the ship was on fire. He hung his clothes himself; brushed down his dinner jacket. He took off his shoes, then he lay down on the bed to read.

*

Hedley Harris took out his watch: just after three pm; the cargo hatches would be closing soon with the last of the mail signed in, less than an hour until they left port. He looked over the paperwork on his table again, the invoices for the fresh produce had come up from the galley, all ticked off. All was in order, but as he stood up to file the invoices, he double-checked the safe was locked. One of the cooks, Minetti, had said that he'd heard a rumour that Mr Davis had made a big withdrawal onshore. It wasn't of any concern to Hedley – he was only the purser, just a seaborne bank teller, all told, a young fellow only at the beginning of his career, and not one for the scuttlebutt of galley staff – but Mr Davis had seemed somehow upset; quietly distressed. There was the matter of the divorce, of course – that would distress anyone – but that had been brewing for years, so gossip also said. There was something else troubling Mr Davis, Hedley was sure, some more serious burden beyond hurt pride or heartbreak. A business difficulty, perhaps. He hoped his health wasn't failing.

'Excuse me, Mr Harris – isn't it?' a woman asked at the window.

He recognised her when he turned and saw her: it was Miss Everley's ever-present travelling companion; he must have seen her half a dozen times at least over the past few years, but he couldn't at this moment remember her name. She was heavily made and plain, but he recalled she had a musical laugh that reminded him a little of Florence, his wife; lively blue eyes. They were about the same age. He smiled. 'Yes, madam? What can I do for you?'

'Miss Carson.' She smiled back at him in her pleasant way, some trace of mischief about her, intelligence in those lively eyes; she was forthright but warm. 'I'm wondering if you might do us a bit of a favour.'

'If I can, I will, Miss Carson,' he replied. Nothing was too much of a favour for Miss Everley or any friend of hers: her father was one of the wealthiest men in the state, if not the nation, and a generous man, too, so anyone would tell you.

'Well,' Miss Carson continued, leaning on the counter, 'there's a young man aboard, tall, fair, possible Scots accent, and we're bursting to know who he is – in fact, we want to grill him over dinner. Could you have a word with the dining steward tonight, please, and have him steered our way?'

'Of course.' Hedley Harris looked down as if distracted by a speck of lint on his sleeve. There was something odd about that passenger that scratched at the edge of his thought, something unconvincing in his rudeness, something – what was it? It was strange that such a gentleman would travel so lightly and without a servant; not unheard of, but unusual. He was relatively new himself to this Nor'-West route, having been with the *Koombana* less than a year, but he was generally familiar with the men of wealth who travelled by steamer – just about around the entire continent, too, from Perth, Adelaide, Melbourne, Sydney, all the way up the east coast to Cairns on his previous posting – and he'd never seen or heard of this one before; not that that meant too much, either, when wealth could be made or lost in the blink of an eye. Still, there seemed something not quite right about this passenger. 'Sinclair,' he told Miss Carson, recovering his smile. 'The gentleman is called James Sinclair. On his way to Broome, I believe, an investor of some kind. No doubt, he will be delighted to dine with you.'

'Ha!' Miss Carson rolled her lively eyes and went on her away again, with a, 'Thank you, Mr Harris,' over her shoulder.

He watched her walk away, the border of pale, rose-coloured lace at the hem of her skirt the last of her to disappear back through the doors of the saloon, and then he stared at nothing but the brass rail on the wall. He stared until it disappeared, too.

It struck him unpredictably, this weird arresting of time. What provoked it now? That queer Scot, Mr Sinclair? Mr Davis's puzzling woe? Perhaps neither. Who would know? Hedley knew the bottom of it, though; he knew where this paralysing shiver came from. The ghost of the *Yongala* sat on Hedley's shoulder all the time, he supposed; perhaps it always would. She was lost in a cyclone off the coast of Townsville, almost exactly one year ago today, all souls lost. One hundred and twenty-two, on the list at least. He'd been meant to be on that ship. He'd been on board her, here in Fremantle, when the word of his transfer had come through, on an afternoon, just like this. He couldn't have been more pleased to receive that news: although he would remain purser, it was a significant promotion: the *Koombana* was the jewel of the Adelaide Steamship Company's fleet. While the wreck of *Yongala* had yet to be found. He refused to think of his old colleagues as gone; they were still away at sea.

Then the ship's whistle blasted for departure, thrusting him back into his boots; they were pulling out of port. He'd go and find Braxton, the steward on dining-room duty tonight. Who wouldn't want to dine with Miss Irene Everley? Besides, Hedley Harris wanted to find out just who this James Sinclair was, too.

*

Fin woke from his doze; he stretched and rose. He stepped over to the window and opened the louvres. The masts of fishing schooners swayed in their docks, sleepy metronomes in the lowering sun. The whole of the harbour was touched with gold – the tops of the quiet waves, warehouse roofs, the bulging folds of sails at rest, the tips of seagull wings – giving him one sweeping glimpse of beauty just as he was leaving, a vision of things as they ought always to be just as they were not. He rubbed his eyes: story of his life, really.

MIYA

Life is accidental, the consequence of endless trails of random circumstance, both miraculous and monstrous, but the laws of life are fixed. All chance occurs within a tight woven matrix of rules. A cloud, floating across the sky, might appear to be a vagrant arrangement of dust and mist drifting and shifting together momentarily but it is formed by the ageless, perpetual dictates of temperature, pressure, volume, gravity. And without the cloud, life would not occur at all. Without its rain, nothing could be made to grow; without its lightning there is no fire – no first spark of being. Without light, without its fire and its eternally resonating warmth, there is nothing at all. Tragedy is to imagine that these rules might somehow be escapable, that one man, one cloud, might ever act in isolation from the rest, from the fabric of existence. That is simply impossible.

I exist, just as do you, by these laws. I grew, just as you did, from the original dust, from the light made of blackness that rent apart the air and the sea to shape this world inside its universe. I settled in the warm, shallow waters of life, the pool of all being, and there I slept for millennia before the fire came for me. I don't remember the storm that brought me to the rock that I would awaken upon, but I remember the pain of coming into this form, this shape. The searing heat, the stretching and splintering of every filament as my first shell was laid around me. I don't know how many shells I had become, billions possibly, one after the next, through the rising and the falling and the cooling and the warming of the seas, until the dust came to change me again. The tiniest speck stole its way into the shell, in under my flesh, and when I couldn't breathe it out, the heat began again, and I began to lay down more shell, layer on layer of bright-hot shell over and over the intruder – *inside* me – until the dust and I became one. Ten summers I kept becoming this way, a globe growing round with layers of light. So you see, it took as long to become me as it has done for you to become you, as it has done for this world to be as it is now.

As everything has been and will be forever.

When the boy found me, when he scraped me off the rock and brought me into the air in his cane basket, I knew I was changing again. His name was Warlitj and he did not know what he had done; he could not have known what was about to happen. He was just a poor boy diving for shells, doing whatever he had to do to survive. His spirit, his soul was so bright then; so easy to sense and to see; he told me within a moment every story he knew. For centuries his family had dived for shells along the coast and had traded them far and wide, inland to the desert, and to the people who came across the sea from the islands, but they'd been pushed off from their trade when the pearl masters came, first chained as slaves and compelled to dive for them, and then driven away from it altogether, to live as beggars. Warlitj had only found his way onto a lugger this day, onto one of the vessels belonging to the pearl masters, because a certain Captain Matheson's Japanese divers had both died in the last week, from the deep-water seizures.

'Wally, get over here,' the captain had called him along the jetty and onto the boat. 'Come out for a dive. I'll pay you in shell.'

Captain Matheson hadn't expected that the boy would bring up much, he wouldn't take him out far, it might not be worth the effort and it was only early in the season, but he didn't want to lose out completely over the days or weeks it might take him to replenish his diving crew. It wasn't easy to get new divers – from Japan or Manila or Makassar – with the policing of non-white workers getting tougher every season. It was necessary to pay a contractor to bring them out – most often a contractor in Singapore – and then there was all manner of paperwork to be done to satisfy the authorities. It could take more than a month if there weren't workers waiting and ready to go up in Broome. Maybe the little blackfeller, Wally, would bring up enough to keep things going, Matheson thought, at least pay the renewal fee on his licence that was due. If the boy did all right this day, maybe they could go out for a week or two, up east off the coast at Spit Point. However things went, Matheson had had no intention of paying the boy in shell or otherwise.

Warlitj knew that but he was still hopeful of impressing the captain. To work on one of the luggers was his greatest hope: he could provide for his whole family on a diver's wage; he could buy meat for his whole family for a year if he got a bonus for bringing up some really good shell. Just to get work cleaning and sorting the pearl shells would have meant the world to him. It wasn't far-fetched: he'd heard of some blackfellas down south at the place they called Cossack who practically ran their own lugger for the big bosses. If you could just get a go to prove you were good at the job, you could make some money and do what you liked with it. He'd show Captain Matheson he was a real diver. He didn't need the heavy helmet and jumper that the Japs wore when they went down, he didn't need an air pipe; only a rope to tie him to the lugger. He knew, deep down through all the long, slow time it had taken to become him, that it was better to listen to your body, to let it tell you when the pressure of the sea became too much; listen to the sea, too, so you might hear if the giant stingray was coming to sweep you away with his great wing. The Japs, with all their fancy gear, would be fooled into thinking they could dive and dive all day, and dive too deep. Warlitj once saw a Manila man pulled up already dead – he'd had a seizure there in the water, his helmet no use against the weight of the sea. It was a hard life for them, for all the Oriental divers, but it wouldn't be for Warlitj, he was sure.

He told Captain Matheson that the best and easiest shell beds were on the shore side of the reefs not far out beyond the great sandbar that sat at the north arm of the harbour, and the captain had laughed, 'Yeah all right, we'll go there,' as if he didn't care much for the boy's opinion. But Warlitj knew, like a map stamped into each speck of dust that made him, that there, below the reef, was a sheltered ledge where the best shell always hid, in the warm shallows. The luggers never went there because of concern over running aground on either the sandbar or the coral, and worse, having the jagged rocks atop that ledge rip open their wooden hulls if the tide whipped out beneath them. Matheson would go there today, though: he was wise enough to gamble that the boy might just be right, and greedy enough to take such a chance. He anchored as near to the reef as he dared and said to the boy: 'Go for your life.'

Warlitj swam out from the boat with his basket and his rope, towards the reef; he did not have to dive deeper than four or five fathoms here and it was all so easy. The fine white sand made the water a little cloudy, but it also made the green of the coral garden only more beautiful, as if it were gently breathing out a mist about itself. Crimson and turquoise parrot fish darted amongst it, while angelfish sailed like slow spearheads made from shell. The boy brought up five baskets full of the real shell that might deliver him from poverty and uncertainty: feather oysters, so we were called, saltwater clams by another name, or Pteriidae, all the size of a man's hand spread wide.

And I was just one of a hundred or so lying there in the sun, on the deck. Even through the hard, rough corrugations of my exterior, the sensation of the air was intense, stunning me at first from any sense of pain; the sea leached and leached away from me, and I could do nothing to stop it. I could feel my life draining away, my spirit pulling away in want of the sea. I trembled there upon the strangeness of the timbers.

'That's enough,' Captain Matheson shouted out to Warlitj when the fifth basket was hauled up and tipped onto the deck. He didn't want the boy to over-exert himself and die, too – not for any care for him, but because Matheson had had to deal with enough death lately. The extra paperwork involved whenever there was that kind of incident was an annoyance to him, and it had to be completed even for blacks these days. He told the boy when he, too, was back on board the vessel: 'You can start opening that lot now.' He'd get these shells sorted for nothing as well.

The tip of the knife slid between the tight-shut edges of me, forcing me apart. I could do nothing to fight it. The light that was me rushed out and the light of the bare, bright sun rushed in and all around. My spine cracked as I was rent apart. My flesh screamed. I knew then that all I had known of life up until this moment was gone.

I had become only the pearl.

The boy looked at me and I felt his wonder as a new flame. He recognised me for what I was, and he was torn two ways: he should take me straight to his grandfather or throw me back into the sea, such was my value. To Warlitj, I was sacred, rare beyond any price, and in that first recognition, he gave me my name, he whispered it into me, 'Miya,' for my light appeared to him like the radiance of the moon; he should take me straight to the elders, who would sing for rain to come through me, out onto the red, dry land. But just as he wavered, just before he was going to pluck me from the shell and hide me under his tongue, the shadow of the captain appeared above him on the deck.

'Christ, would you look at that.' He grabbed me from the boy.

And it was at this moment that my change became complete: in the absence of shell, I began to lay down my curse around me.

For theft unleashes a law of life, too. Tragedy is the thief who denies there must be recompense against his greed. It was simple. I would be used as I had been made: to call the clouds over the land. Or I would be returned to the sea. But to steal me, to keep me from my purpose, is to pay the highest price. To pay with your life.

By the time Mr Davis decided finally that he must have me, eleven such payments had been taken; and two more were owing. Seven years and seven new names had been endured. It's not as though I hadn't given ample warning of my intentions. I could not have made it clearer if I could in fact have written it in stone or howled it across the ages.

Still, I felt sorrow for that one called Mr Davis, this last in the line of thieves, this one who only wanted love; who only craved that essential warmth from which all things come. And so he would have it, although not as he wished; perhaps not as he deserved, either. As his ship pulled ever closer to me, I felt sorrow for him and all who were with him, all who were innocent. From my black box, as yet so far away, I begged him to change his mind, just as I begged him to come ever closer, to take me, to cast away his anguish and throw me back into the sea.

There was no other way that this could end. It would end when the next moon, now waning, fell black.

IRENE

So much for dazzling this Mr Sinclair with my entrance – he's not here when I slink down the staircase and into the dining room, late, quarter-past eight. I feel a little silly somehow, schoolgirlish. And miffed, as if he's stood me up. The place is only half full, too: no-one else here to impress.

At least my other motive for late arrival appears to have had the desired effect: Marg and Mr Davis are pleasantly ensconced together when I spot them just to the other side of the vase of palm fronds in the centre of their table. They're sitting opposite each other, chatting away over their glasses – that's nice. Her citrine bracelet is twinkling sunshine under the electric light as she smiles deeply into whatever it is he is saying.

'Miss Everley, isn't it? Good evening.' A man catches my elbow before I can join them, pinching the hinge of my tortoiseshell armlet right through the top of my glove and into the tender crook. I blink over a tiny, silent yelp of protest as I turn to him. It's the captain of this ship. Captain Tom Allen – inveterate sea dog, Adelaidean, all moustache and shiny buttons, married to the job. I've only met him the once, coming the other way, last September, just after he took over as master. He's a darling of a man but about as interesting as a wet sock, that way the very cautious and conscientious invariably are.

'Yes. Good evening, Captain Allen.' I give his sleeve a squeeze in return, mostly as an entreaty to him to ease his own grip – he has hold of me as if I might float off out the window otherwise.

'So good to see you again.' I smile as he finally lets go. *Please, don't ask me to join you.*

He won't, though: I see over his shoulder that his table, here at the head of the room, is full. Full of wet socks. There are a couple of fellows from Public Works, and a pearl rattler, wife of another government someone, but I can't recall her name; beside her is the chief officer, whose name escapes me, too, and at the far end of the table are Mr Spark, who owns the groggery at Derby, with one dog-collared reverend I've never seen before, two West Kimberley cattlemen who could talk ticks and natives for Empire, and another pearl rattler, who I think is the mother of one of the Public Works chaps from Broome. Oh, and beside her, there's Corporal Buttle up the very end: Derby policeman and prison warden in one handsome package – shockingly handsome, actually, and as spectacularly dull. I'd have to put the fiction engine into full steam to write about that lot.

'Your father was in fine form when I saw him last – when was that, January we would have brought him home?' Captain Allen goes on genially.

'Indeed you did.' I nod and smile. 'And now it's my turn to head that way.'

'Safe home again you shall be soon enough, Miss Everley.' I suppose he is smiling through that enormous moustache. 'It's a pleasure to have you aboard.'

He turns back to his table, and I'd be on my way, too, only I am immediately caught at the other elbow; I feel a small, sharp shoulder lean in to mine with a slight roll of the ship. 'Irene. Irene Everley – good heavens, how long has it been?'

Long time for me to get to my table. I wave over at Marg before turning to the source of this further delay. I've noted already that the voice does not belong to someone I admire, and when I see her face, it's confirmed. It's Suzette Leighton, nee Meade. Also Adelaidean. We met on several occasions while I was at university – she's the sister of Desley Meade, who pipped me for a first in the final Modern European History exam – and by a horrible twist of coincidence, she more recently married an old rugby chum of Marksy's, Wynne Leighton, so that I was forced to re-meet her in Melbourne last year. She's the last person I would have expected to see here.

'Suzette. Good heavens indeed.'

Her eyes dart about all over me, taking in every inch. Careful, both memory and instinct warn: she's a viperous little thing. She is a gossip and a snipe: if it takes one to know one, I know this one too well.

'What are you doing here?' she asks me with faux friendliness, but it's an inquisitorial probe, as if I'm the one who doesn't belong in this scene.

'On pilgrimage to dear old Dad,' I reply, and signal over at the steward who is hovering at our table with my entrée; *yes please*, my downward pointing finger tells him, *put it there*, as I add to Suzette: 'The question is, what are you doing on my patch?'

'Your patch?' She laughs with faux humour. 'You don't look over it very closely, do you? Wynne has been out here on business, seconded to the Bank of Western Australia since the new year, presently in Broome, wherever that might be.' As if she doesn't know; and as if the very idea of not knowing where Broome is doesn't make her sound like an idiot. 'We hardly ever get five minutes together, he's always so busy, and so I'm on my way over to spend the winter with him. How could you not have known all that?'

I know Wynne is probably dreading winter a little. Marry for money repent every penny – tsk, tsk. I sigh and don't need to pretend to be cool with her. 'Oh, it's hard to keep up. Must catch all the news later, if you'll excu—'

'How's Edward?' she needles on regardless. 'Have you set a date yet?'

'Edward?' I laugh: no-one calls Marksy 'Edward', except perhaps his grandmother. Edward Marcus Densforth – Your Honour, Supreme Court Justice – is his father. Marksy, the son, is Marksy, or Marcus at a stretch, and barrister only because it wouldn't do for him to strut any other sort of stage. I say, 'Suzy, you funny old thing. Marksy and I aren't in any hurry.' I stick her one back: 'But tell me, have you and Wynne managed any breeding yet?'

Her face is the mask of evil, carved in primordial stone. That one hit home so sharply for a second I regret having said it.

Until she replies: 'Wynne and I aren't in any hurry to end our honeymoon, you know how love is – or do you? It must be difficult to turn your mind to marriage when you have so much else to think of – so much harder for a woman to have a career *and* love.'

'A career?' I give that idea all the horror it deserves, as my heart skips a proverbial. How could she know about my *Aus Life* scribblings? She can't. Impossible. Only Marksy and Marg know, apart from my editor, Phil Oswald, hard-boiled misanthropist disinclined to indulge himself in the kind of rubbish that sells his papers. I'm not even on the payroll, officially. The ludicrously tiny sums I'm paid per piece get remitted directly to the Perth Children's Hospital. Suzette is bluffing, surely. Fishing. She'd damn well better be. I tell her, and I'm not lying: 'I dream of finding myself one, one day – a *career*, that is.'

'Still?' Her smile is thin-lipped with insincerity, with a grasping, desperate need for superiority, and now *she* dismisses *me*. 'Well, I mustn't hold you up anymore, Irene. Yes, let's catch all the news later, shall we?'

Unavoidable, I have little doubt. God save us, how long will we be sharing ship? Ten days? Minimum – let the tides and sandbars be kind, I pray as she turns away, slithering back to her companions in the far corner. They have their backs to me, but I know who they are: Alice and Gennie Skamp, stepdaughters of the Pearlers' Association big wheel, Sydney Piggot, and just about the extent of the female complement aboard. I resist the urge to dash over and alert them of the she-snake in their midst; they're not stupid, though, or married, either – Alice must be two or three years older than me, and despite her beauty, she's seen no need to have herself shackled. I don't know what the sisters do with their time, though, other than not being married, and being a bit wet-sockish themselves, if wet socks can be a little over-starched and terribly, terribly ladylike, and now I'm annoyed with myself for giving it any thought. For letting Suzette Leighton get the upper. She'll keep, won't she. I shall immortalise her in caricature and see it circulated fifty thousand times across the eastern states. I'll scratch out a couple of notes on the back on my menu card in a moment.

'Was that that Suzanne Whatshername?' Marg asks me when I at last make it to the table; she met her briefly in Melbourne on a couple of occasions, too, and came to her own judgement.

'*Suzette*.' I give her a thin-lipped gargoyle grimace for yes indeed, as Mr Davis springs up to tend to my chair beside his, which of course is fixed to the floor and that brings a hot prickle of shame to my cheeks: some people can't help being decent even where there is no need, and pride themselves on being seen to be so; it's as ingrained and animal as spikiness is in others. My own spikes jab at me, and out of me, at my walls; my skin screams out at my confines. I shoot a manic glare at the bottle of wine on the table, willing it to pour itself into my glass, because I can't pour it myself here: I couldn't embarrass Mr Davis by doing so. Oh, God, but I've got to get out of here. As I swing round in the chair and tuck my knees under the table, the loops of the gold braid that edge the cloth wink across my lap, looping round and round and round, and I could tear the whole thing off the table with my teeth, just out of this frust— *Arrrrrrgh*! Marg is absolutely right: one day I'll do something truly destructive unless I break free.

'Goodness, I'm thirsty,' I give Mr Davis his prompt, and as he pours I rip off my gloves, asking him and Marg both, 'So, what have you two been nattering about, then?'

'My daughter,' Mr Davis answers, with that distracted sadness under his tired smile. 'Dorothy. She has just turned seventeen, and I miss her. I miss my son, too, of course, Gerald, but he is busy at school – busy not writing me enough letters, as boys do. With a daughter, well, it's different. I can't expect her to spend the season in Broome with me, as I would like her to, as if she were still a child – she must begin to look towards her own future – but she's in Sydney, you see. She is so far away, and it seems further away with every hour.'

Mr Davis seems far away. For all that I must agree with him that Sydney is a disappointment generally – a fishbowl on a larger scale, where princesses compare waterfront yardage, rather than measure themselves in lengths of pearls – I realise Mr Davis is lamenting that his daughter is not only in Sydney but with the mother. And probably the mother's lover, too. His sadness turns my stomach and my mind over at once. No marriage is perfect; my parents bickered – Mum calling Dad irresponsible, Dad calling Mum a whining pain – and I still think one of the reasons Mum left the way she did was because of all the worry Hal caused her out on the station, the breakneck, single-minded way he goes at everything, the waiting for word, waiting for him to reappear, the mending of wounds he'd bring home for her to fix – she'd had enough, did the ultimate walkout on him. But I can't imagine infidelity, how devastating it must be. Probably because I've never been faithful. I have faithless, meaningless midnight assignations with other women's husbands instead. I drain half my glass in one go.

'I know,' says Marg in that cajoling way she has, when she's about to suggest a game of cards or charades on a rainy day. 'Why don't we go shopping – in Broome, no, Port Hedland. Tigs,' she turns her bright smile to me, 'where did we see those beautiful Pilbara rubies last time? That mad little Syrian hawker in – where was it?'

For a moment I don't know what she's talking about. I shrug and look down at the sliver of salmon before me: with shame that I probably won't eat it. Unfortunate fish, on my plate in vain. I throw down the rest of my glass and smile across at Mr Davis to refill it, but he is looking intently at Marg.

Her topaz bracelet twinkles as she waves towards the window at the black sea beyond the end of our table. 'Wherever it is, I say let's find something lovely for you to send to Dorothy – for no reason other than to remind her of your devotion, and to remind her of home.'

'What an excellent idea.' Mr Davis actually smiles, the first time I've seen him do so this trip. We'll fix his glumness – or Marg will.

She rolls her eyes, her pretty, sapphirine eyes, and she laughs her pretty laugh. 'But perhaps not pearls.'

Pearls, pearls, ubiquitous Nor'-West pearls. I touch my own slim string of seeds, which I wear almost always, because they're Mum's and Dad bought them for her before they had any money to speak of, fresh off the boat from jolly old England, young hearts full of wide blue dreams, well before I came along, and I laugh with Marg and Mr Davis. 'Yes, cheers to that – anything but big fat clacketty clacking pearls, hm?'

Mr Davis fills all of our glasses and, still chuckling, he declares: 'Pearls have probably ruined my life!'

'Oh come on, enough of that, now now.' Marg won't have him return to the doldrums.

Neither will I. 'You have given your family a wonderful life care of them pesky pearls, dear Mr D. Never forget that.'

'This is true, Miss Everley.' He nods slowly, at all his faraways. 'My family has plenty of money these days. But I have spent all these years going back and forth, back and forth – from Broome to Melbourne, from Broome back to London – never stopping for long enough to *be* a father, *be* a husband. How can one have a family and live like this? It must change, this I know. I must do something else.'

As much as I might understand that sentiment, he's blaming himself for his wife's behaviour – and that won't do. I'm about to touch his hand, clenched as it is on the table beside mine, and tell him no, this is not your fault, even if it is, when Marg shifts the mood again.

'Yes, why not sell up and change your direction while you can? Too many are ruined by pearls one way or another. Perhaps they're all cursed.' She says this almost fiercely, and she's speaking particularly of her father's ruin, I know. It's not an irrelevant suggestion business-wise, either, though: Mr Davis already has other investments; he has at least one stake in some Kimberley property that I know of, not to mention the renowned 'De Vahl', his palatial digs on Roebuck Bay; he can do what he likes. But then Marg says: 'No really, perhaps there's something to it. The number of stories one hears – well, even in that imbecilic magazine I was reading this afternoon – what was it? *New Century Woman*? That thing was worse than *Aus Life* – anyway, in it, there was a tale of a bedevilled pearl. The Blush of Death – it brings doom to all who possess it. Ridiculous, gratuitous piece designed to keep housewives in a state of general alarm even in their moments of leisure, but there wouldn't be so many stories about deadly pearls if there wasn't some truth, don't you think?'

I think Mr Davis suddenly looks appalled. I'm sure I do, too. For such a sensible woman, Marg does occasionally coast dangerously close to the ridiculous herself. I'm not sure what Mr Davis is reacting to here, if perhaps she's touched on some sort of religious or intellectual objection to the occult, or to stupidity, or both, or he's more simply taken aback by the over-heated high pitch of her voice just now, but I shall endeavour to rescue the conversation.

'Marg.' I give her a good dose of quizzical eyebrow. 'That wine has gone straight to your head.' I say to Mr Davis: 'Marg has never been much of a drinker, you know – this Moselle is lethal stuff.' And back to Marg: 'There is no such thing as cursed pearls, and you don't believe in any such thing, do you.'

'I believe in evidence,' she replies, raising a cautionary eyebrow back at me, and she's not the slightest bit drunk – she hasn't taken a sip from her second glass at all. Mine is apparently half-empty again.

Mr Davis is pressing the edge of his napkin to his forehead; his perspiration is glistening under the light. Perhaps he's unwell, rather than disturbed by our conversation. Dear man, he has had such a bad time of it. This persistently revolting weather can't be doing him any favours, either: the fans whir, the ship clips along, the windows are all open to the night and still the air is thick. Mucky. I'm about to ask if he's all right, when the catch-pin slips from my pearls, sending them on a breastward slide, just as the steward attending our table leans down to discreetly interrupt us. 'Excuse me, ladies, sir.' He tells me in particular: 'As you requested, I can inform you that Mr Sinclair has arrived.'

FIN

'Miss Everley and Miss Carson have insisted on your company, sir.' The steward on duty at the dining-room door smiled at him, pointing the way to their table, handing him a menu.

'Oh? That's a pleasant surprise,' Fin replied, but he was more curious than surprised. Which one was she? Miss Everley or Miss Carson? Either way, a substantial part of him didn't really care. Despite his doze this afternoon, and because of it, he was weary – he'd missed lunch. He glanced at the menu: salmon and cucumber sauce, sweetbreads a la St Cloud, sirloin of beef, fillet of veal, ice cream, lemon meringue, raspberry mousse – he would eat well for the next little while. He'd have preferred to eat alone in his cabin, but he thought that might rather have the effect of drawing more attention to himself by his absence. He hadn't wanted to enter the dining room too soon, though: it was always best to move among others when they were busy, eating and chatting, and possibly two glasses in. Always best to hide in plain sight, up to a point.

The room was small, as he had expected it to be; it would seat seventy or so when filled to capacity, but this night there were perhaps only forty here. No heads turned as he made his way to the ladies' table – he'd certainly timed this well – but his senses remained alert. He looked closely at all he saw. The wealth in this room was not conspicuous; he'd noticed over the past few weeks that the further west one travelled the more difficult it was to judge the status of people, not that judging an Australian on appearance was ever easy. One man at the captain's table wore an ordinary summer suit of linen, as if he'd just washed up on some nearby beach, but he probably owned the beach. There was a quiet, understated elegance in this room, too, compared to the saloon at least: it was all graceful palm leaves and warmly polished oak – that was, until he noticed the tablecloths. They were green, the colour of billiard baize, and trimmed with gold. A casual touch of Christmas in sweltering, tropical autumn, a contradiction upon a contradiction that challenged the observer not to be chipper at every odd thing.

'Good evening.' He approached the table, resting a knuckle on the edge of the billiard baize. 'I believe I am to be seated here? I apologise for my lateness.'

'Late? I've only just arrived myself,' she said as she turned her head to look up at him.

And as she did he couldn't conceal his astonishment at her beauty. He barely heard the exchange of names that followed. Miss Everley. Irene Everley. He'd been preoccupied when he'd glanced at her in the saloon this morning, when he'd met her gaze in the reflection of the bookcase glass, but now, so close, it wasn't so much the arrangement of her features as an attitude. It wasn't the colour of her hair, which was fair and fine, and not unlike his own; it was the way she wore it, promising that it would soon cascade down her back. It was the way her earrings, delicate, filigreed leaves of pale gold, almost touched the curve of her neck with their pointed tips as they swung, but not quite; the way she reached out her hand to him, the self-possession he saw in her striking amber eyes: she was positively feline. He recognised her straightaway, as of his tribe, and the fire between them was instant. She engulfed him.

'Excuse me a moment.' Her voice was slightly rasped, slightly laughing, slightly indifferent, but clear in every word, strong, her smile a dare as she withdrew her hand again to fix the clasp of her necklace.

'And you must excuse me, please.' The man at the table stood. Davis, he'd said his name was. Middle-aged, he wore wire spectacles and an expression that might be read as hurried or harried; his moustache was not too neatly kept, nor the hair on his head, but his dinner jacket was of the best quality. A businessman or lawyer, perhaps, or a scholar of some kind; whatever he was, he seemed a man under some burden of worry, carrying a weight of thought or care. 'I must retire,' he patted his pockets as if to check that he was in fact here at all. 'The first night at sea invariably has me laid out.'

'See you again, I'm sure,' said Fin, with mechanical courtesy, as he sat down, and the plump one beside him, Miss Carson, underlined the man's exit. 'Poor Mr Davis. He's not feeling very well, is he.'

It all meant nothing to Fin.

The woman, Miss Everley, looked over her shoulder after the man as he made his way to the door. 'Yes, I'm a little concerned, too. I've never known him to be seasick.' And then she turned back to Fin, those earrings swinging. 'He's a dear old friend. But you, on the other hand, are a complete mystery. Who are you and what are you doing here?' She challenged him with a slow and crooked smile that played with him as she searched.

'I'm on my way to Broome,' he said, letting himself return that smile, that look.

'Broome.' She mimicked his accent. 'You *are* a Scot, aren't you. Where from? Glasgow?'

'Yes.' He laughed. She was a student of character, it appeared, just as he was, although he thought he could safely presume their motivations were quite different. 'Well picked,' he said.

'Well, what do you know, this ship is from Glasgow, too,' the plump one put in. 'Built for speed and shallow water.' She sounded a little daffy in the blithe, offhand way she spoke, but he suspected she was far from it; she was taking his measure.

'Marg, really.' Miss Everley was not inclined to heed her friend, he saw. 'So what has brought you to these fair climes?' she asked him across the table; she was leaning her chin on the palm of her right hand, exposing the bare white flesh of her arm, inviting him to look at her, and look at her he did. The ivory lace at the front of her evening gown gave the illusion that her breasts were bare, too, beneath a draping of gossamer, some fabric that wasn't quite a colour at all; wasn't quite substance. She was clothed in the same material that made dragonfly wings.

'Business. Boring,' he told her, giving her the lie of why he was here, and he flirted a little, with his eyes, and with his smile, to distract from his business, yes, and because he could hardly suppress his desire. 'Or so I thought it would be.'

'Hm,' she said, glancing away at the bottle on the table, deflecting, too. 'I think we need more wine, don't you?'

'Not for me,' he said, flirting a little more. 'I don't drink.'

'Oh?' She was intrigued.

'A promise I made my mother, long ago.' He intrigued her a little more with the truth. He had promised his mother, for all the suffering brought to her by her common, streetwalking destitution, he would never be common himself; he would never be an idiot like all the other lads, either; he would never waste a farthing pissing it up a wall.

'Good for you.' She glanced away again. 'Marg? Will you have another wine?'

'Ah, no.' Her friend frowned, pulling her chin in like a nanny rousing on a child. 'None for me, thanks.'

'Ah well,' she said as a steward arrived with plates of main course, 'I suppose I shall have to do something sensible then, such as eat dinner. Oh look, beef, peas and spud. How very yum-yums. How very surprising.' But as the steward placed the meals on the table, she instructed him: 'I'll have a Tom Collins, please – not too heavy on the fizz.'

'You and your Tom Collinses,' the friend roused again, and then she looked square at Fin. 'He was a mystery man, too, you know – Tom Collins. Have you heard of the hoax?'

Fin shook his head, although he'd heard the story of it once or twice. He let her tell him.

And she did, pointing the tip of her knife towards him as she spoke. 'It began in New York, so the story goes. Someone would say to an unwitting acquaintance at some bar somewhere, "Have you seen Tom Collins?" and the acquaintance would say, "No. I don't know anyone by that name." Then the trick would be played: "Oh but Tom Collins knows you – and he's been saying all sorts of dreadful things about you." Such a mean trick. There's no such person as Tom Collins, of course.'

'Marg, you are full of fascinating nonsense tonight, aren't you?' Miss Everley cut into her sirloin, taking a sliver of it onto her fork, nudging three peas then onto the back of the prongs. Everything about her was fascinating.

'You can count on me, Tigs,' Miss Carson replied.

'Tigs?' he asked, seeing an opportunity to turn the conversation away from himself. 'What's Tigs stand for?'

'Stand for?' Miss Everley raised her fork with the question. 'It's just an old nickname,' she answered, her cheeks flushing a little. She really was exceptionally beautiful, this Irene Everley. She possessed the kind of beauty that could very quickly relieve a man of substantial portions of his brain. 'My family calls me Tiger,' she explained, and he fought to keep his attention on her words. 'My father has always called me Tiger, ever since I can remember, for my supposed fearlessness, wherever I might have misplaced it these days. Anyway, at school it got shortened to Tigs. Marg and I were at school together, you see.' She turned to her. 'I dare say Mr Sinclair won't remain a mystery for long. We shall pick him apart between now and Broome.'

'And I look forward to it.' He smiled once more under a nod; she would unravel him in five minutes if he didn't keep his head. *Tiger*, he smiled deeper still: he could see how she got that name. It was the way she looked; those amber eyes: she was a white tigress. She would tear him apart.

'Do you have a nickname?' she asked him as her drink arrived.

'No. Jim – does that count?' he said, all his names crowding in again. *Jim. I am Jim. James Sinclair*, he forced that name down with a mouthful of beef. He would kill Jim Sinclair when he left this ship behind him; there had never been any such person, not really.

'Jim? Hardly.' She laughed. 'All right, next question, Jimbo. What exactly is your business in Broome?'

His reading this afternoon had given him his story, and it rolled out of him as any lie ever did: 'I'm off to inspect a lugger I'm considering investing in.'

'A *pearl* lugger?' Miss Carson's voice was so shrill it rattled off the overhead fan.

And Miss Everley ignored it. 'Why a pearl lugger?' she asked him. 'Are you a sailor or a fool?'

'Both.' He laughed; to invest in a single-schooner operation was a high-stakes risk, he had read only a few hours ago, and no doubt one a naïve new arrival from Britain with a little money might well be attracted to, as a moth to a flame. 'I mean to say, I was a sailor, yes,' he explained. 'Royal Navy.'

'Ooh. So you are a salt. What rank?' She bit her lip in anticipation.

'Lieutenant,' he gave her the lie there, too, but he'd used this one so many times in the recent past it almost felt true; he'd never been promoted beyond able seaman, and given his background, an officer rank was an impossibility. He'd gone into the service at sixteen, as a fair portion of the lads from Braefield did – it was either the navy or the shipyards or more or less direct to prison – and being a pretty boy, the initiations among the ratings were typically unpleasant, with his life advancing only in terms of further degradation from there. Nine years, almost. He bit down on the bitterness of every second he had endured. Survived. 'I was with the Mediterranean Fleet,' he lied yet again, to muddy his tracks; he'd been with the East Indies Fleet, transferred then in '04 to the Australian Station. 'Battleship, gunnery.' At least that was fact: cannon-fodder-in-waiting; they all were, should any actual battle eventuate. 'HMS *Avenger*,' he said; there was no such ship: he'd served on the *Goliath* and then on the *Psyche*.

'Why did you leave your commission?' Miss Carson asked, and even though it was a rude question, he smiled at her, almost sincerely. She was only protecting her less guarded friend, but he let his eyes convey his disappointment, in her, and in the answer.

'Medical discharge,' he told her. 'Malaria, at Suez.' He'd spent time in infirmaries over those nine years in the service, but never for a disease. 'So I came out here to recover my health. It worked. I'm perfectly fit now.'

'Is that right?' Miss Everley teased; the way she looked him over let him know how well aware she was of his physical fitness. He made a habit of being so, and was a little annoyed that this ship, for all its luxury, appeared to carry no gymnasium, and probably no sporting equipment apart from the requisite skipping rope and a few sets of quoits. He imagined holding Miss Everley up against the wall in his cabin instead, her thighs around his hips.

'Yes.' He laughed again, over the stirring that began in his tackle for it right now, as their smiles curled together across the table, one inside the other. 'I'll most likely be returning to the navy soon, if they'll have me back,' he told her, signalling their time was brief. 'I imagine I'll transfer to the Royal Australian, though, since I am here, enjoying these fair climes, and she is her own fleet these days.' In fact, he'd read a few weeks ago in some paper that the *Psyche* was presently with the RAN in Sydney Harbour and of course he wouldn't be going anywhere near her, or that harbour ever again.

'So, Mr Sinclair, Lieutenant Sinclair, you're a bit of a wanderer. Just like me,' Miss Everley said, and he could see that she recognised something of herself in him, too. He could feel her own restlessness, her own wanting, and regret flickered in him, for he could never rest, no matter how much he wanted to. And he did want to rest, sometimes with a desperate need that came upon him as a sensation of pain, a fist pressed hard into the centre of his chest.

'You must tell me about your own wandering,' he said, and he turned his attention to his meal.

As the two ladies talked, one over the other, of their endless trailing to and from Perth and its awful weather, its flies and humidity, the horrors of Derby cattle country, the smog of Melbourne, the dust of Adelaide, he let them imagine he carried his own weight in his silence; that they had touched on some inexpressible sadness in him after all. There was no surer way to get a lady to shut up with all her questions than to let her believe he was wounded. He was only thinking what easy lives they led, though. How protected and cushioned they were; removed from the everyday, moving about as they wished. He watched Miss Everley play with her dessert when it came, reducing the mound of raspberry mousse to a pink sludge; he lit her cigarette.

'Anyway,' she exhaled, and the smoke swirled around under the fan, 'that's about all I have to say for myself, I'm afraid. I do nothing. I go nowhere, not really.'

And he knew in that moment, in that *not really*, that she was a liar, too.

'Well, well, what do we have here?' Another woman appeared at their end of the table, right at his shoulder. She was small and stringy; pinched – like a hungry mouse. 'Suzette Leighton, Mrs,' she introduced herself to him, and he to her, then she said: 'Irene Everley, Miss, ever with a dashing chap, isn't she – Mr Sinclair, didn't you say it was? Shall we all go up to the saloon? Have a turn round the piano?'

'No. Not for me,' Miss Everley gave this woman a cold and suddenly sober stare. 'More like time for bed, I think.'

'Oh, that doesn't sound like you, Irene,' the woman with the pinched face protested. 'Life of the party, you are.' She turned to Fin, her spite as sharp as her pointed little nose. 'But her fiancé is just as bad.'

'Not tonight, Suzy.' Miss Everley stood abruptly, Miss Carson, too, and Miss Everley made a show of a yawn. 'Perhaps some other time.'

Fin stood also, of course, thinking: *Fiancé?* And that only made Irene Everley more desirable. It wasn't the idea of bedding another man's woman that got him running hot – for all his deceit he was too honourable for that sort of thing – it was the idea of bedding a rich man's woman that stirred him again now. Almost irresistible.

As she brushed past him with her, 'Good night,' she whispered, 'Number twenty-three.'

Fin coughed into his hand to avoid responding. He wasn't going to rendezvous with her, not really. This was not the time for complications. Intimacy was too dangerous; he was too frayed, too tired to trust himself with more than a dinner's worth of conversation, never mind what a good grinding does to a lady's need to know – everything. He reminded himself: two weeks and he'd be on his way out of the country. And two weeks on from there, he'd be on a beach somewhere, with a Javanese maid, or a Tahitian princess. Enjoying women in port had never been a problem for him.

He watched the women go, heading for the staircase; most in the dining room were doing the same, or preparing to. Honest people, he thought, at least most of them would have been. People merely going for a song in the saloon, or a cigar among the blokes in the smoke room. Fin longed to be, more than anything else, one of them. Just an ordinary, honest man. Would that ever be possible? Possibly not, he thought. Not really. Java or Tahiti, wherever he went, he'd always carry this weight of lies. Too bad, for some. For him.

When he took a step now to leave, too, to return to his cabin, he felt something slip across the toe of his shoe. He looked down and saw what it was: her string of pearls. A string of tiny white pearls, a tiny trail of pale tiger light sprawled across the deep-green carpet.

He picked them up, he put them in his pocket, and then he left the dining room. He walked up the stairs and out into the night.

*

Abraham Davis heard a knock upon his door, and answered from where he sat at the writing table in his cabin: 'Yes?'

'It's only Evans,' came the reply. Abraham's new secretary, John Evans, come up from his own cabin, on the deck below, in second class. He barely knew the man yet, but he was very helpful, very efficient, very serious about himself – Welsh. 'Is there anything I can do for you before I turn in?' he asked, waiting there in the corridor.

'Er ... One moment.' Abraham rose from his chair, from the letter he was writing to Rabbi Lenzer. It was a rambling, so far pointless missive, mostly on the state of the weather and various mutual acquaintances in Perth; a letter saying everything except what he needed it to say: that he felt even his faith slipping away from him today. Abraham de Vahl Davis was a pillar of the East Melbourne Hebrew community; he had been president of the synagogue board up until all of this travelling had made it impractical for him to continue; even still, he conducted Saturday synagogue himself all through the season at his home in Broome. Yes, the divorce had humiliated him; yes, he hated Cecily like a stain on his soul; he hated that the children still loved her; he hated that she remained their mother. Yes, he was weary, sinfully despairing; yes, he felt he had failed his children, his community, and he had failed God. Yes, he was resentful that his brother-in-law, Mark Rubin, his business partner, never left his London townhouse these days. But none of this could justify what he was about to do. He knew it was wrong, legally and morally, he knew that it was confused thinking on his part, but he believed, if he purchased the pearl, he could regain control over his life, he could be master of his own ship again. He couldn't tell any rabbi that.

He even had a buyer in mind, in New York, one who he was certain would offer $125,000 for it and all its curses; converted back to pounds, that would give him a profit of at least £5,500 on the original £20,000 outlay. Then, once he sold his portion of the business back to Rubin, he would have enough money altogether to start afresh, without losing out, to anyone, ever again. He would build his business on his own terms, perhaps even go fully into real estate and grazing, and not a whole continent away from his children.

But the compulsion ran deeper than all of this. Just the thought of touching the pearl, this legendary pearl, sent a strange excitement through him; ever since he had received the telegram this morning, from Neath, up in Port Hedland, telling him 'Rosy' had finally surfaced and could be his for £20,000, he had felt it was his destiny to claim it. To hold it, even for a short while. To call it his. To break all curses as he enclosed it within his hand.

A voice had told him, deep inside and with such compelling clarity, that the only real evil laid upon this pearl was the fact that it was stolen. He reminded himself that he'd never broken a law in his life. Perhaps that was the problem. Perhaps it was simply time to dare. To break the rules – just *once*. Indulge in his own affaire de coeur – the only way he knew how. With a deal.

Whatever it was that had got into him, a further flash of clarity now told him that the real insanity was that he had £20,000 in cash in the ship's safe and no-one but himself knew it was there. He usually only carried a maximum of £2,500, for incidental dealings at Shark Bay or Cossack along the way back to Broome. But £20,000 in floating cash? This was careless; he could have a heart attack and anything could happen to the money. Not that he didn't trust young Hedley Harris, the purser, but he didn't want to pique the lad's curiosity, either; it was more sensible that his secretary, who had come to him so highly recommended for his discretion and professionalism, should know the precise amount he had deposited in the safe, that he be given clear instructions on its disposal should anything happen – dear God, but he felt as if he might have a heart attack any moment.

And so he replied to Evans at the door now, 'Yes. Do come in. There is something important I must discuss with you.'

*

It was well past ten pm, possibly heading for eleven, when Fin returned to the promenade deck. He'd been losing time scoping the ship, roaming the main round the cattle stalls and the galley, where one of the cooks had been locked in battle with a stewardess over the urgent need for some lady or other to have a jug of boiled milk taken up to her – 'I'll do it myself,' the stewardess had griped. 'And would you look at the filthy state of the saucepans here.' Her weariness had heaved out into the night, and Fin had envied her that complaint. He'd made his way then back up to the spar deck, round the accommodations of second class, past the empty dining room and the twin berths of first beyond, taking the stairs from there back up to the superior staterooms, where he would find number twenty-three, portside, and starboard, his own cabin, too.

Music drifted from the saloon, along under the promenade awning, some love song about silvery moonbeams and wandering dreams. The moon this night was in its last quarter, a sickle glowing softly behind a film of cloud, and the air was still warm; soupy. Perfect, so Fin thought.

He still didn't know what he might do when she opened the door. Irene. He wondered if Miss Carson shared a suite, or a connecting cabin; what she might see or hear. Nothing, Fin decided. And in the same breath, he wanted everything. He also considered if he should, more importantly, keep that string of pearls pocketed. What were they worth? Maybe £50? Or £5? He had no idea, but it would be a few bob. It would be useful.

'Yes, it is cash.' He heard the words slip through the louvres of the first stateroom door he passed along the internal portside corridor, and, although he couldn't see through the half-closed slats, he was sure it was that Mr Davis he'd met in the dining room earlier; a clipped voice, somehow worried and impatient, something Continental about it. Fin stopped, instinctively, to listen.

'Cash is necessary,' the voice went on. 'The Malay dealer will not accept a cheque, of course, and it was necessary, too, that I make the withdrawal this morning from Fremantle as it is not always easy to obtain that quantity of cash in the Nor'-West at such short notice. The whole sum in the case is twenty-two thousand, five hundred; however, the smaller amount is for ordinary, incidental purchases. Only the package of twenty thousand is for the purchase of the three new schooners, which, it is hoped, will have arrived in Broome by the time we dock there, fully equipped. If anything should happen to me for any reason – and if the schooners are not at the jetty in Broome – you are to request that the purser release my case from the safe into your custody, and you are to deposit the cash immediately back into my account with the Union Bank, unless of course I instruct you otherwise in the interim. All of this is understood?'

'Understood, Mr Davis, very good, sir,' another man said.

'Yes, good,' Davis replied. 'I will give written instructions to this effect to the purser in the morning – telling him that you will have sole access to my case in the event that I am for any reason indisposed.'

'Sir? Are you fearful of that happening?' the other man asked with concern. 'Are you unwell at all?'

'My word, no!' Davis laughed, but it was a mirthless sound. 'Although this infernal humidity might kill me soon. I must attempt to get some sleep. If you will please leave me to it.' Fin could hear his voice moving towards the door, a trace of a lie recognised fake to fake, and he began to walk on his way.

Who carries around that amount of cash? Fin wondered as he walked. It was true that he didn't know much about how business was done in the West, but it seemed somehow blatherous to him. A bank in Broome wouldn't have a spare twenty grand in the safe, with all the trading that went through there? That didn't seem plausible at all. A small slice of that number might be nice, though, he supposed, imagining a note or two falling from a stack of crisp ones and into his hand. What must it be like to truly be a thief, to think that way? He asked the black waves through the night. To be so cold. He still had hope that he would never know. But hope is so easily surrendered to practicality, to opportunity; he knew that far too well.

He stood now in front of cabin twenty-three, and he knocked on the door.

MIYA

While the laws of life are fixed, while the natural consequence of theft is immutable, it is not always easy to perceive who or what is the thief.

For example, when the great-grandfather of the boy Warlitj first speared cattle on the Pilbara, he and his fellow hunters did not consider their actions to be wrong. How could they have been acting in any way other than in accordance with the law? The creatures had been let loose on their land, land that they did not possess by virtue of any government decree but land that they believed possessed them. The cattle were loose on country the hunters were inextricably responsible for protecting. Some of the cattle they speared were eaten, of course, feasted upon, and the skins and bones were useful, too, but many more were culled because, in such increasing numbers, they were destroying the creek beds that reached towards the desert, and those creek beds were vital in taking the rain further than the clouds could go. And yet the hunters, when caught by the cattlemen, would find themselves in chains, or dead. In turn, they speared the cattlemen; and in turn again, the cattlemen shot or poisoned or chained many more of the hunters; stole their women, too. The cattlemen, with equal ferocity, reasoned that the land belonged now to them – as this was their law, and their belief.

Where is justice here? Where is the law? It can be hard for one man to see. Whole empires rise and fall in tides too vast for him to track, and if it is he himself who has been stolen, dispossessed, he cannot even see the tracks of his own making. I can see so much further than a man and it is difficult for me to judge. I can trust only the weight of the chain. My light is wounded by the black iron that is clamped around the neck of the innocent, my light searches out the depth of his sorrow; I hear him cry across all time, even in his most secret silence. But I can do nothing to cure his injury. I can only destroy my own thieves. I am as trapped as he is in this bind; and as fierce in my desire, my scalding need to be released. Fiercer.

If I had been taken from the sea for a purpose other than greed, other than empty, lustful wanting, other than a spiritless exchange for the nothing called money, then events would have unfolded differently. If Warlitj had been allowed to carry my power to call the clouds into the desert, I would not have needed to destroy so many; I perhaps would not have destroyed anyone at all – certainly not deliberately, and only ever those few unfortunate souls destined to be taken in a storm, as happens from time to time anyway. If Captain Jock Matheson could have perceived the shock and fear in Warlitj's eyes as he stole me from the boy, if he could have perceived his own mistake here and relented, I would not have needed to destroy him, either. If he had not been so cruel to the boy, in refusing to pay him even in shell, perhaps I would not have been so cruel in reply.

Oh, how I tried to return to the sea, but Jock Matheson would not let me go. Just as he was holding me up between his thumb and his finger, holding me up in the shade of the foresail to see my colour, one of the crew – his name was Tami – felt the hairs rise on the back of his neck, sensing that some bad thing had happened. He looked over at Warlitj, who sat hunched by the pile of shells on the deck, as if he had been kicked. Tami didn't know Warlitj well but, being Makassan, he felt a deep-rooted sympathy for him. The people of Makassar, across the Timor Sea, and all the peoples of this land, from Marapikurrinya, here at what had now been called Port Hedland, all the way up to Kununurra in the very east of the Kimberley, had traded with each other for centuries before the pearl luggers came – they exchanged shell and women for cloth, tools and tobacco. The Makassan people came

into this shallow harbour to hunt trepang – sea cucumbers – and
they had sometimes fought with the Kariyarra and Nyamal people
who lived here over where they could fish, but they, too, had been
pushed off by those such as Matheson. Pushed off and made little
more than slaves themselves, always paid less than others, always
at the mercy of less scrupulous masters. So, when Tami saw Warlitj
hunched there, I called on that long history and that sympathy, I
sang to Tami's instinct to cause him to pick up one of the main
mast ropes that lay on the deck, just behind Matheson's feet, and
pull it sharply around the back of his ankles.

I had wanted to topple him over the low deck rail and into the
water – me with him – but he did not even stumble. He shoved me
into his trouser pocket and stepped over towards Tami by the main
mast, smacking him across the side of the head, as he told him:
'Idiot. Watch what you're doing.' Then he shouted to the whole
crew – Tami and two others that there were: 'Bring her in!'

Once back in port, Matheson set off for the Pier Hotel, to start
drinking rum, not only in celebration of the big beauty of a pearl
he told himself he had found, but because that was his custom
whenever he was on land. Each step along the jetty he took, I
willed him to trip, to smash into the water, but he did not. It was
a hot, still night that night of the new moon all those seven years
ago, in the March of 1905, and, as Matheson leaned on the bar to
order his first drink, Warlitj disappeared into the falling darkness,
into the shadows that stretched behind the hotel. The boy reeled
and staggered as he ran through the sandy laneways of the town,
overcome with guilt and fear – if only he had not hesitated at his
instinct to hide me in his mouth. I tried to communicate to him that
it was not his fault, but he could not hear me; he did not recognise
my voice in his distress. I could not so much as raise a whisper
of a breeze to try to show him, either, I was too new to myself
then; I did not yet know my power. And he was soon too far away,
running towards his mother, his heart full of shame and his pockets
empty, running to her shelter in the scrub on the furthest reaches of
Stingray Creek. He was just a poor, stupid blackfella, that's what
those who held power over him had always said; and now he was
beginning to believe there was no other way for him to be.

At the same time, in the furthest corner of the saloon of the Pier Hotel, two Chinese watched Matheson get drunk. Lucky Yong and Han Wang Chao had their own long history with this place, and as they watched him, I watched them. By day, they traded in gimcrack – counterfeit gems – which they imported from Singapore, and cheap shell they bought from several of the dealers here, all of which they ran inland via an Afghan cameleer, who would hawk it off to lonely cattle-station wives. These Chinamen hoped to make as much money as they could before the authorities inevitably came for them with fists full of deportation orders, and lonely outback wives weren't their only victims. By night, they did their more lucrative trade – in stolen pearls and shell. They had been discussing which pearler they would target next when Matheson walked in with a swagger. What about him? They wondered together, wordlessly. What had he brought in today? When I saw their thoughts, I sang to them with all the force I had then and my own distress: *Steal me.*

As I sang to Matheson, too: *Have one more drink, and one more.*

'Yeah, I got myself a beauty this arvo,' Matheson began bragging to another at the bar, his voice loud, his mind scrambling with the rum. 'Must be sixty grains – maybe sixty-five. She's fucking big and fucking pink.' He grabbed me out of his pocket and raised me to the light of the kerosene lamps that hissed above the room. 'Look at the colour. My Blushing Bride,' he called me. 'Have you ever seen a pearl as fucking pink as that?'

His associate cautioned him then, but merrily: 'You better put that fucking big pink thing away, Jock – how many times you gotta be told to keep it in your trousers?'

As all the men at the bar roared with laughter, Han and Lucky overheard someone say, 'Shit, I reckon she'd go for a thousand quid, easy, once she's clean,' and at that moment, they set their sights on me, this Blushing Bride.

The Chinamen knew Matheson, of course – they bought up his waste shell, scrubbing and chipping it to ornament steeped and stained teak trinket boxes they passed off as sandalwood inlaid with Mother of Pearl – and Lucky, the more charming of the pair, went over to congratulate Matheson on the find.

'Don't think you're cheating me out of this one,' Matheson slurred. 'You tricky little yeller feller.'

Lucky was also the more ambitious and impulsive of the pair and easier for me to convince. Cheating was soon not what he had in mind for Matheson.

During the pearl season, Matheson spent his nights onshore in room eight at the hotel – everyone knew that – and a few hours after last drinks were had and the place lay in silence but for the snoring and farting of drunken sleep, Lucky Yong and Han Wang Chao crept in through the kitchen at the rear of the hotel, up the stairs and along the hall, where they slipped the lock on Matheson's door. Then, inside, while Han moved about in the dark, quick fingers searching for me, the pearl, Lucky stood over Matheson with his knife raised.

Han could not see the knife, busy as he was, first hunting for and then through the pearler's clothes. It had been agreed between the pair that Lucky would render Matheson senseless with a rag soaked in chloroform – they'd done this sort of thing on half a dozen occasions before.

But that was not what would happen this time. I ached so hotly for this revenge, it had grown into an agony of need within those first hours of my time in the air, and I screamed: *Kill him!*

Kill him now! I demanded, and Lucky slit his throat.

I took no satisfaction in his death. He woke, just for a few seconds, as his life drained, and I could see that Matheson had been a lonely man, the cowardly bullying son of a cowardly bully, and that he had no real friends to speak of. He summered in Geraldton alone in a small house that had once held promise of something else: a wife who had died five years prior, giving birth to a son who had died there, too. I pitied him all his tribulations. But I felt no remorse for having killed him. He had made his choices. He had deserved to die.

I was not so sure of this at the time, however. Rage and grief and pain confused me, even as my purpose made its first strike. Back then, when I was so new, I did not have much understanding of what I had just done – nor what I was about to do.

CLASP

In the forests of the night ...

IRENE

Disgrace is the shape of my smile as I open the door – I know it's him. I caught the scent of his shaving soap as it wafted in through the louvres on this thick, lazy breeze a moment before he knocked. Lieutenant Sinclair for supper. I have written myself sober for it – and he is delicious already.

'Oh?' I'm not altogether feigning surprise as he stands there against the night. Grecian god, hands in his pockets that slouch to the left. Take me to Olympus.

'Miss Everley, do forgive me for disturbing you at this hour,' he says, begging not for forgiveness at all. That accent – I am rolled up inside his rhotic consonants. 'I believe you dropped your pearls.'

'Did I?' The Chantilly edge of my camisole enquires from between the crossover folds of my kimono; the centre of my tulip swells.

'You did.' His smile is all boyish hope and cool assurance at once; yes, he knows why he's here. How could he not?

'Perhaps best not to linger at the threshold, making a spectacle, hm?' I suggest. Suzette Leighton's maid has been scurrying about, up and down the corridor, up and down from shearage, so known on the *Peapod* for the bulk carriage of shearers ever there below. And all such scribbling thoughts are now suspended. Let's not be distracted now. No.

'Hm. Best.' He steps into the cabin, glances around, at the bed, the sofa, the washbasin; at my unpacked clutter strewn over all: my array of toilette, silk stockings hung over the wardrobe door, my blouse from earlier this afternoon fallen to the floor by my typewriter, still yet boxed inside its black leather case; a half-demolished tin of Plaistowe's Westralia assortment on the bedside, minus all of its walnut creams, stray wrappers fluttering around my notebook like slovenly little angels under the draught of the fan. He appears to be taking in every detail; he is a cautious fellow.

And I promise him: 'We're quite alone.'

I take him by the lapels and pull him to me, counting round my monthly likelihoods again, cursing the absent preventative, then re-convincing myself it's safe enough, and not caring at the same time: I've done this on too many occasions before without event, I've long suspected I'm barren anyway.

He tastes of salt and, curiously, I'm sure the hint of soapy cologne is Canadian Alpine Snow emollient – a shilling a jar. Such an ordinary, workaday scent of man, but on his skin – I want to lick it off him, all of him. The taste of conquest – oh yes, my whorish vacuity disgusts me, and this is the last time I will behave this way. Absolutely the last. I'm going out with a bang.

'Miss Everley ...'

'Irene.'

'Irene ...'

'Shh.'

I drop my kimono to the floor, and grasp the front of his shirt to begin the popping of studs, but he stops me, his grasp gentle yet firm around my wrist. He whispers: 'Easy, Tiger.'

And he pops his own studs, slowly, fixing the backing links to each as he goes. Silently. He makes me want to scream. He places the shirt studs in the little china dish below the dressing-table mirror, and they plinkle around the Adelaide Steamship Co insignia there; they are silver, uncommonly understated, plain but for a tiny bird in flight impressed upon their faces.

Next, he meticulously unpicks the knot of his shoelaces before slipping them off, nudging them precisely beneath the sofa. He hangs his belt over the scrolled arm, his trousers too, along their creases. I could watch this nightly. This musculature is all taut ropes; this naked thigh, sinews flexing as he bends, has me mesmerised.

At last he shrugs his shirt from his shoulders, and if I was in a state of arrested rhapsody a moment ago, I am somewhere I've never been before now: an old scar runs around the top of his right arm, time-bleached and jagged. A thousand stories flood me. A bar-room brawl; a bloody battle at sea, dreadnoughts at fifty paces; secret agent sent to spy on the emperor of Japan. Certainly not malarial fatigue and early retirement to the antipodes. I want to know who this man is – every last inch.

I take him with such hungry violence my wanting turns the iron bedstead beneath us to dust, to steam, to stars.

FIN

He gathered her afterwards into his arms, and there upon his shoulder she fell into that lovers' repose, that twilight between dreaming and reality. His breath against hers, rib to rib, he held her. He watched her float and drift, and he wondered where she went, what fantasies carried her. He wondered also at her sadnesses, at what losses had brought her here, for he was sure that only some yearning, some absence or some aching need could explain her careless abandon. Why else would such a woman – wealthy, beautiful, bright – risk herself this way? She was somehow drowning there in his arms, and the only shame was that he could offer her no rescue. Within the fortnight – in fact, within ten days – he'd be gone from her world; he would never see her again.

'Hm. Salty.' She smiled into him with her eyes closed.

'Salty?' he asked her, unsure what she meant, if she was referring to some taste or to the sex.

'Hm. You are. The saltiest salt ...' She moved her hand across his chest.

They rested there together like that for a little while. The sea was calm beneath them. The fan above them swept on and on; the engine shushed them along below. He watched the pulse at her neck; he watched her finger play among the soft, fair hairs of his chest. He was sorry; he was always sorry for the girl, whichever girl, when it was finished.

'I should go now,' he said.

And she said, 'No, don't.'

'Yes. I should and I must.' He gently pulled away from her and rose from the bed. 'Too many eyes on a ship such as this. Can't say I was returning a strand of lost pearls all night long, can I?'

'You can,' she said, leaning on an elbow, those amber eyes wide awake once more, following him to the settee, to his clothes there. 'Never mind too much propriety on my account, Mr Sinclair.' She laughed at herself deprecatingly.

But his bristles let go for a second at her lack of care; the lack of care only the very rich can afford, for they live so far above the engine room. 'Too high for judgement, are you?'

'Too high?' She laughed again. 'Nothing but a low-class lush from Aussie here. No-one really cares what I do – that's what I was getting at. Well, that is to say, my father would be devastated at the half of it and Marg is permanently appalled, but don't be fooled into imagining that breeding could be of any consequence to anything other than cattle where I come from.'

He chuckled at that. She was magnificently bred: she was everything about Australian women he found attractive: so free. So often bold. And more: he'd never met one quite like this before.

And then the sadness fell into her eyes again as he began to fasten his shirt studs. 'Please, don't go,' she said. 'Not yet. I want to find out all about you. Who are you? Really.'

His sadness matched hers, for all she'd never know; for all he didn't know himself. 'We have ten days,' he told his shoelaces; he would tell her nothing. He would develop an awful and unfortunate case of the flu overnight and be confined to his own cabin for the rest of the journey. He looked up at her again from where he sat on the settee, lacing his shoes: he was so sorry. But he said nothing.

He stood and took the pearls from his trouser pocket. 'I shouldn't forget to give you these now, should I.' He coiled the string into her hand, holding it by the clasp. 'The catch is twisted – a little bent.'

'I know,' she said, and she held his gaze. They held each other in that gaze, so joined in this recognition, so peculiar to them, as if they'd known each other in some other life long ago. He knew the details of her face as he knew the details of the clasp he held between his thumb and forefinger: studied once, etched forever. 'I should have it seen to.'

As she said this, turning from him to place the pearls in the bedside drawer, he saw the profile of her breast, soft and round, the nipple raised as if it still beckoned his kiss, and any resolve he might have had to keep himself away from her evaporated.

He told her: 'I'll ask one of the engineers for a toolbox in the morning, see if I can fix that catch myself.'

She grinned in conquest. 'Handy *and* salty.'

'And dangerous.' He warned her as he played along.

'Well, aren't you perfect, then.' She watched him over her shoulder, over the soft, round rump of her hip, as he moved towards the door.

'If you say so.' He smiled as he left her. 'I can be perfect for the next ten days.'

And no more, he told the night.

*

Hedley Harris watched from the portside rail, amid the hush of the first-class staterooms here, where he was enjoying his end-of-day pipe. He would usually watch the stars from this spot, sending his goodnights to Florence and baby Jack, out over the stern. But tonight the clouds had blurred the view, and so, his eyes wandering idle as his thoughts, he was staring back towards the aftmost entrance to the accommodations, when he thought he saw that strange passenger, James Sinclair, come out of one of the cabin doors, just inside in the corridor there – nowhere near number eleven, the cabin that had been assigned to him this morning.

It was dimly lit this time of night, only a dull bulb remaining on above the entrance, and he stood at a distance of perhaps fifteen or so yards, but he was sure that it was James Sinclair he saw, striding away down the promenade, a certain gait, a certain air, black suit quickly one with the dark. With the safety and security of passengers always front of his mind, the purser now moved quickly to that cabin door – number twenty-three – and every step increased his alarm, on recalling whose cabin that was.

'Excuse me, Miss Everley?' He knocked. 'It's Harris – Hedley Harris, the purser. Are you all right in there?'

'All right?' He heard her move towards the door. 'Of course – is the ship sinking?'

That mocking drawl of hers – languid, bored and provocative all at the same time – always tightened his throat; he imagined few men would be immune to its effects.

She opened the door in her dressing gown and he concentrated most determinedly on the tip of her nose to prevent his eyes from wandering anywhere else.

'Yes, Mr Harris? To what do I owe the pleasure, then?' There was a hint of annoyance in that which confused him – had he woken her up? Had he been mistaken in thinking that he had seen Mr Sinclair leave through this door a moment ago? From where he had watched, back towards the stern and with the distance, the angle of his view had perhaps given him a false perception. But hadn't he heard a door close there? Perhaps the man had left from number twenty-one next door instead? Miss Carson's cabin? Surely not. Whatever the case, this was all most embarrassing. Perhaps the man had simply been going for a walk.

'My apologies, please, Miss Everley.' Hedley Harris did all he could not to trip over his words. 'I had thought I had seen a man leaving your cabin. But clearly —'

'Mr Sinclair?' Her laughter cut at him, a blade rasping through silk. 'Dear fellow was just here – returning my pearls to me. I dropped them in the dining room. Don't worry – I fought off his advances with my lethal ju-jitsu skills. He won't try it again.'

'Miss Everley.' Hedley Harris backed away. 'Again, I apologise. I have intruded upon you unnecessarily. Please accept —'

'Oh, Mr Harris, please, please *you*.' She smiled, and the tone of her voice was as sincere as it had just been derisive. 'I appreciate your concern. Very much. Thank you.' She closed the door. 'Goodnight.'

'Goodnight, Miss Everley.' He stepped back out onto the promenade, and looked down its empty length, into the black of the night, the black of the sea. There was something he did not believe here, something amiss, he was sure, and at the bottom of his unease remained the question: who was this stranger, Sinclair? He would talk to Corporal Buttle in the morning about it, suggest to him that he might want to keep an eye on this one. Or would that be a little excessive? An overreaction to a suspicion he could not yet even name? Something was telling Hedley Harris no: if this man was some sort of impostor – an impostor who might well have begun to ingratiate himself with Miss Everley – it was best he act. Leave hesitation to lesser men and act now.

MIYA

I hadn't understood that I had only poured oil on the fire by letting my need for revenge rush out from me the way it had. I hadn't understood the train of destruction that had been set in motion. How could I have known? I did not know what it was to die; it's a concept that even now I struggle to comprehend, for it is something that I can never know myself.

But then, who can truly know death other than those doomed to believe that every story must have an end?

The bloody gasp of Matheson's final breath struck into the heart of Han Wang Chao with such a force and with a barb sent so deep he would never free himself of the sound. Han was a cheat and a liar and, at his very essence, an indolent man of wasted intellect, but he was not a murderer. He had almost dropped me when he realised what Lucky, his partner, had done. Almost. Han was too conscientious in his thieving, if little else, to loosen his grasp on me. Against the wild roaring of his own blood in his ears, he wrapped me into the jewel pouch he always carried and slipped back out through the darkened hotel, back out into the night.

You fool, you hopeless fool, your stupidity knows no end, the words of his father wove around and around his horror at what Lucky had just done. Han, so I could see from the stories that spun from his soul, was the third and youngest son in his family and had been born sickly and small – useless from that day forward as far as his father had been concerned. His father had been a boatwright, a hard man, respected in his trade, and disgusted by any weakness. His mother had urged young Han to go to the monks at the Jade Buddha Temple in Shanghai, to do something with his cleverness, to study with them and perhaps earn a chance to become a scribe, but that had seemed a prison sentence to him – twelve years ago. Monasteries were places for the unwanted, he had thought. He'd run away from home then, just before his thirteen birthday, he had run as far as fate could take him from Jinshan on the shores of Hangzhou Bay, but he could never run from his father's contempt. Not any more than he could run from this distress now, this gathering regret, here on this Pilbara shore at Port Hedland.

Lucky followed him out, and when they were far enough away from the hotel, he hissed through the night at Han: 'You got the pearl? You got that red pearl?'

Hong Zhen Zhu, this Lucky Yong called me in his language, a sound as soft as the plash of waves on the sand below the piers of the jetty that struck out into the bay, and I felt the jolt as he grabbed Han by the shoulder, spinning him around.

'You killed him.' Han shrugged him off and kept on his way. By habit more than sense, he was going to the shack, their tin-and-canvas hovel that sat behind the clutter of shell-packing sheds that stretched towards the beach. 'Why? Why did you kill him?'

'I don't know,' Lucky said, hardly caring for the answer himself, still under the power of my curse. 'Because he deserved it. Why not kill him?'

'What's got into you?' Han stopped and stared at his partner. After more than eight years of this petty, predatory existence they shared, there was not much respect or friendship left between them, but there had been a trust, of sorts. A predictability. And now? Han was struck by a deeper horror still: what had it all been for? Over these years, he'd amassed a small fortune of more than a thousand pounds, which lay rolled in an old flour tin, buried in the clayish sand under the floor of the shack, never spending a penny more than he had to – unlike Lucky, who spent his on whores and cards and opium. The cash was as meaningless as everything else inside this lightning flash of realisation. Han couldn't do anything with all his money: he had no family to send it home to, no wife, no chance of being able to do anything with it in Australia, either, buy a house or build a respectable business, not with the laws the way they were against the Chinese, and getting harsher every day. And now this new low? Murder? He shoved Lucky in the middle of his chest, as if to push at this reality, demanding of him again: 'Why? Why did you do this?'

'I don't know,' Lucky could only reply once more. 'I heard shouting in my head and I wanted to kill him, so I did. Why are you crazy about it, Han? No-one will care about Matheson. The Red Pearl will make us too rich – it's as bright as the moon. A blood-red moon.'

'You are crazy.' Han started on his way again. He was going to get his cash and get on a foreign lugger tomorrow; get out of here, get back to Singapore, anywhere, and then? It didn't matter, so long as there'd be an ocean or two between him and Lucky. Han was still a young man – only twenty-five – he'd settle down, find a wife, find a home, maybe send for his mother if she was still in Jinshan, break the chain that held her to his father, break all his own chains, spend the rest of his life repairing his mistakes – go to the monastery if that was what it would take to clean himself of this. Murder? *Murder?* He could not believe what Lucky had done.

'Give me the pearl.' Lucky kept on behind him. 'I want to see if it glows in the dark.'

A camel brayed a way off behind the foreshore sheds where the Afghan caravans were waiting for the next steamer to pull in with its load of drapery and tableware from Adelaide, tomorrow afternoon. The hawker Abdul Alameddin would wait there for Han and Lucky, too, to fill up his jewellery drawers with rubbish to sell out at Marble Bar. Tomorrow, instead, surely the police would come for them – they would come for Luck Zhang Yong and Han Wang Chao with a noose. A shouting began in Han's head: *No. No. No. No. No.*

I whispered under the shouting: *Hong Zhen Zhu is yours – I am yours. I am the fabled Ming Yuey, the magical pearl of legends. Lucky Yong has betrayed you. Take me, and you will be free of him. You will be free in every way. Give me to your mother, and you will be forgiven everything.*

All I wanted was for him to fight with Lucky. I wanted them to grapple in the sea, where, once in the water, I hoped I might find my way out of Han's pocket. How I might go about unwinding the cord that wrapped me in his silk pouch, I did not know. I did not know then how the water would empower me; all I knew was that I had to find myself there, in the sea. I had to find my way home – and *I* would be free.

'Give me the pearl, you cock,' Lucky Yong demanded, as Han strode on.

Lead him down to the water's edge, Han. Lead him away from the sheds so no-one will see or hear you teaching him the lesson he must be taught. Show him how you feel. Now. Free yourself from him.

But my hopes were thwarted again. A long-handled fishing harpoon, which lay propped upon the rocks at this point along the beach, caused Han to trip in the darkness and stumble to the sand – and when he did, Lucky Yong was on him. There was not much difference in them to look at: they had the same kind of physique, slight and wiry, and similarly angular faces, which they had used often enough to confuse westerners, sometimes purely for their own amusement. It was one important difference between them that counted at this moment, though: Lucky's greater confidence, his certainty in his own superiority. He might not have been as intelligent as his partner, but he was twice as arrogant. And this arrogance gave him twice the strength. A street-brawling urchin escaped from the wharves of Guangzhou, Lucky was always the brawn, always the one to subdue any threat, the one to press the chloroformed rag to the mouths of their victims and drag them into the shadows, and occasionally, hold the tip of a knife to a neck. Now a killer, he held the tip of that still-bloodied knife to Han's.

'Give me the pearl, you cock.' He was in every way insane. I had made him irretrievably so; I could do nothing to stop him.

The more I screamed for the safety of the sea, the more determined Lucky became to possess me. He had murdered for me; he believed he had paid the highest price for me. I would be his.

He grabbed the jewel pouch; I felt the heat of his hand near scorch the silk that contained me. He stood, and looked down at his partner still lying there in the sand. 'Don't disobey me again.'

Han remained silent. He watched Lucky begin to walk up towards the sheds, his shadow-shape beginning to take colour in the first glimpse of dawn; and then he stood, too. He picked up the harpoon and ran at Luck Zhang Yong: he drove the spearhead into his back; he felt the barbed edge scrape the spine.

Lucky made no sound as he fell to the sand, or none that I could hear above my screaming, my desperate plea for release. Shouts of horror certainly rang out loud and clear across the town of Port Hedland in the morning, when first Lucky was found, and then Jock Matheson up in his room at the Pier Hotel. They thought a psychopath lurked in their midst – maybe an Aborigine gone wanda, or maybe a pearler with his brain too starved of air. They thought that someone had lost their mind.

Someone had: Han Wang Chao. He lay in hiding at the back of one of the shell-packing sheds, behind a high stack of empty canvas sacks. He lay there hiding with me, clutched in his hand. He had convinced himself that so long as he possessed me, he would be free. Because I had told him so. I felt no regret for the ending of Lucky Yong: he was, on balance, probably best gone from this life, best banished from this form; a blackened soul that knew little but senseless want and ceaseless consumption, I supposed he might be better employed as an amoeba feeding on sewerage scum, or sent backwards to the very beginning of time before light. A speck of coal dust. That wasn't for me to decide or to know. But the fate of young Han, well, that was something else again. It marked a hopelessness for us both.

It showed me that I was trapped in this curse as much as any who dared to desire me. *Take me to the water, Han – throw me into the sea. Then you will be truly free.* I begged him; I tried to twist his obsession, harness it to my will; I really did try to free him. To free us both. But he could no longer hear me. His destruction was unavoidable. In my distress, I sent out my light in that dim corner of the shed, searching for an answer, and as I searched, I glimpsed my own future; I saw all the turnings of the earth, the moon and the stars; I saw my curse play out to its savage end. I saw Han Wang Chao, in all his hopelessness, look down at me with his handsome young face, smiling at me as I glowed there in his hand.

And yet I still hoped. Even as I waited for that final hand to come to me, for that last along the line, Abraham Davis, I hoped events might play out differently. By that time, all those seven long years later, I was shut into the black box, locked in the desk drawer of the one called Jarrod Neath at the Port Hedland branch of the Union Bank, and I was infamous. I knew the extent of my power by then, too; I knew all that I had to do. But still I hoped for the one called Mr Davis. As much as I sang him to me, as much as I insinuated my will into all his weaknesses, I hoped that once he found me, by the strength of his good nature, his honour, he would be compelled to throw me into the sea.

Mad, yes, perhaps. But life, even a life so eternally conscious of inevitabilities as mine, is impossible without hope – perhaps my life especially so.

IRENE

'Miss Everley.' The steward arrives at the breakfast table with a tray. It's not my poached egg; it's a pair of tiny pliers on a plate, and a note. 'Mr Sinclair sends his compliments.'

Sending a flash of heat from tulip to cheeks. 'How sweet.' I take the plate from the tray, and the steward scuttles away, too busy to wonder at whatever the game is here.

'Do I detect at last some colour of shame on that face?' Marg asks as she skewers a piece of rockmelon to her fork.

'Shame?' No. I can still feel him within me, full and firm, the head of the bedstead hitting the oak panel of the wall, despite its feet being screwed to the floor. I want him to screw me again – right now. I suppose Marg listened to the whole thing through the panelling between our cabins; difficult not to, and it wouldn't be the first time she's been forced to endure that kind of entertainment. But this time something has given me an odd colour, even if it's not shame. It's – what? Some sense of defeat at my apparently unquenchable predilections? I make a decision to stop this behaviour and my body's response is to redouble its desire. I can barely think of anything else; if my body truly were a tulip, my petals have so fully bloomed they're curling back against the stem, leaving my centre irrevocably exposed. Tender. So wonderfully tender.

I open the note, as I continue to ignore Marg's enquiring eyebrow.

Good morning, Miss Everley,

As promised, if it is convenient, I will call at your cabin to fix the clasp of your necklace at ten-thirty am, unless of course you would prefer to see to it yourself – in which case, you might return the pliers to the Fourth Engineer, a fellow called Christie, when you're finished.

Enjoy the day, whatever it brings,

J.S.

'Tigs?' Marg is continuing to enquire. 'I must say, you don't seem quite yourself this trip, even if you seem only more dreadfully yourself. What's going on?'

'I don't know.' I stand. I suddenly don't feel like my eggs.

'Irene?' Marg's fork clanks against the edge of her plate with her frown. 'What is it? What's got into you?'

'This dragging humidity, I suppose.' Or some kind of god, really. I'm so well slept I feel as though Eros might have taken me on a tour of heaven through the night and left me on a cloud – the wonders of not falling asleep drunk for the first time in weeks, more probably.

I glance at the note in my hand once more: even his handwriting is careful, lacking in presumption, making the power in this all mine. I don't want anything at all but ten-thirty am – but him. How very odd. I haven't felt anything like this since I first met Marksy: Royal Melbourne Golf Club, pre-prandial cocktails, April the 23rd, 1906, a Monday, at approximately 6.20 pm; he handed my stupefied little face a martini and gently disabused me of any notion by telling me he'd long been fond of a Hellenic lass called Margery, and even after he'd finally confided what that actually meant – that his preferences were all and only Greek – it took me a good twelve months, innumerable gin-sodden heart-to-hearts, and three terrible lovers to get over him. But by jinkers that was all fun, too, though. He chased me across the southern extent of the continent, across three states, to make sure I wasn't too badly bruised – the truest lover, of sorts.

'What does that say?' Marg is still frowning, referring to the note in my hand, and pulling her chin in dubiously at the pliers in my other hand. I wish she wouldn't pull her chin in like that – it makes her look like a worried frog.

I shake my head at her query, give her the usual riddling refrain: 'What you don't know you can't tell.'

And I'm saved further probing now with the arrival of Mr Davis anyway.

'Good morning, Miss Everley, Miss Carson.'

I can only smile, 'Lovely morning, yes, lovely day, whatever it might bring,' as I wander off among the tables upon my little bright cloud. What's the time? Almost nine. That's an hour and a half to wait, and, more immediately, to get this smile out of the public gaze: indeed, what has got into me? I'm a grown woman these days, not an ingénue of barely twenty-one. But this face, my face, I am sure is incandescent with happy anticipation – I am fearful I might start skipping in a moment.

I pass Suzette at the bottom of the staircase and my smile is embarrassing – so sincere she frowns sceptically at me, too. 'Good morning, Irene?'

'Oh isn't it?' I beam at her. 'Let's meet for coffee this afternoon – a game of euchre? At four?' Did I just say that? Evidently. I just about sang it.

And she frowns suspiciously. 'Perfect.'

At the top of the stairs, I press my hand to the fingerplate on the swing door here, as though I might ground myself against its solidity, and touch instead the brass impression of a Grecian urn I've never noticed before. My laughter crashes against the heavy air outside, and I gulp it in like a new intoxicant. I am magnified somehow, electrified. Like this air: promising a storm – oh please, yes. Cut me loose.

Once in the cabin, what to do? Switch on the fan and undress, then sit down en déshabillé at the writing desk in the corner by the door and look into the embroidered doily here: an olive grove stitched in sepia needlepoint, the branches of the two trees in the foreground pleached together, Keats' declaration threading through and around me: *Beauty is truth, truth beauty – that is all ye know on earth and all ye need to know.* I want him here *now*. What's the time? Nine-twenty.

To wile the minutes on, I scribble out some more notes for the column, a syrupy subplot of Ishmael of the *Peapod* getting his girl across the breakfast table – across his invariable serve of oats and stewed rhubarb, he asks my Marg to be his wife. Bravo. Oh, God, but I can't call her Marg – scribble that out and she becomes Miss Perle de le Prix. And this really must be the last from B. Sharpe. Any more 'Purple Daze' and my brain will turn to stewed rhubarb. I stab my pencil at the page. Yes: after I've done my duty in Derby, I am going to go to London, I really am. I truly am promising myself this time. No, actually, I'm going to New York. I'm going to disappear into that vast and anonymous metropolis and write very dirty books. I am one of *those* women. I light another cigarette – all I can do to avoid pleasuring myself before he gets here.

When at last he knocks at the door, I just about drag him in through the louvres.

'Jesus,' he says into my hair.

'Wrong room,' I reply, searching for his firmness – *there*. Oh.

He laughs against my ear. There will be no meticulous folding of clothes this time. I take him into me perched on the desk, his shirt as yet still half-buttoned, his white flannel trousers round his ankles. We pause this way, pleached one into the other, and we unbutton his shirt together.

I touch the scar on his shoulder; I grasp it as he begins to move again, and yet some pause in me remains. Something is different now. Something has changed. Perhaps only some lost thing found. Perhaps only some want of love, *this* love, gone unsated too long. But I don't know this man. Why should I want to love him? It's all so very strange.

FIN

'What happened here?' She traced a finger along the scar once more, when they had finished their coupling and lay on the bed, their legs entwined.

Why spoil the fantasy with the truth? That was his first thought. It would be spoiled well enough when he left the ship in Broome; following fast on that thought was a kinder one: he should begin to put her off. Tell her a lie: invent a wife that had come after him with a cleaver; give some hint that the injury was dishonourably acquired.

But the truth was worse than that. Her eyes – bright, questing, so honestly wanting to know – compelled him to tell her some of it. He told the ceiling fan: 'I got a lot of unsought attention in the navy, as boys of a certain appearance do. A senior officer took a particular fancy, but as I wouldn't take that from him willingly, there were consequences – involving a smashed bottle of Bell's malt, intended, I think, for my face. He was drunk, though, and missed. I was seventeen.'

He didn't tell her that his aversion to being sodomised had been well wrought previously at the Braefield Industrial School, or that the 'senior officer' was in reality merely a leading rate called Blocker Blackstone, whose disciplinary methods were only slightly better suited to an insane asylum than to the Royal Navy, or that this scar was among the least that Blackstone had done to him, to cause his service record to be marked 'accident prone'.

'How old are you now?' she changed the subject, seeming to sense other wounds.

'Thirty-two,' he said, those other wounds crowding the room: Blackstone thrashing him with a length of winch rope; Blackstone concealing gravel in his stew; Blackstone ordering him to kneel and grasp the stokehold ladder, taking to the backs of both his hands with a crowbar there, a small audience of those on fire duty at the boilers that day being told that this is what happens to those who frig themselves off. Unrequited affection can be a terrible thing. He could still hear the roaring of the furnaces; see the lads there staring at the spectacle in fear, with their coal-blackened faces shiny with sweat, their mouths shut tight.

'I knew it.' She pressed her body against his side. 'Thirty-two,' she mimicked his accent again. 'I knew you were thirty-two.'

'Did you?' He smiled and held her there. 'What else do you know?'

'Nothing.' She made a show of pretending ignorance.

'Nothing?' He pretended to be astonished, and he thickened the brogue just for her, straight from the streets of Glasgow. 'Nothing won't butter my parsnips, woman. Come here.' He pulled her on top of him; she shrieked out a laugh, making no attempt to be quiet about it.

Astride him now, she demanded to know: 'Where do you live when you're not ill-advisedly inspecting pearl luggers in Broome?'

'Melbourne,' he said, knowing this was slippery – didn't she say last night at dinner she spent time regularly in Melbourne? He knew nothing of Melbourne apart from the few nights he'd spent there, in Fitzroy, planning to leave on the next mail packet to Adelaide. The docks had been busy, a good place to be invisible; there had been a lot of pub talk about naval shipbuilding, work soon to be starting on a battle cruiser and a couple of destroyers, for the new Australian fleet. What else? Men of wealth had seemed to have a preference for tailcoats.

'Whereabouts?' She circled a finger through the hairs on his chest.

'South Yarra,' he said, searching time back to the lie. 'Finlay Street.'

'Finlay Street? I don't know that street,' she said, working her circles down the tight drum of his abdomen. 'I know South Yarra well, though – I have a very good friend who lives there. Where's Finlay Street near?'

'Why? Are you going to look me up when you're next in Melbourne?' He stalled her, trying to find a diversion. But she was the one in command here: her honey-warmth sought him again and she had him hardening.

'I might,' she said, and she took him in, working him so that he wasn't sure if he was dreaming this sex or living it.

'That's amazing,' he said.

'Well, where is it?' she asked him.

And he hardly heard her as she rocked him. 'What?'

'Finlay Street.' She laughed.

'Right here,' he said as her laughter tightened round him.

'No, really.' She stopped still then and lay her palms on his chest.

'Don't ask me to give you directions,' he told her, confused, under a spell that might have been the best or the worst of things, he couldn't tell. He could hardly make sense of anything but the way her long hair fell down around her shoulders, down around her breasts, champagne cascading over skin. 'I haven't lived there more than three months,' he managed to say. 'Ask your friend where it's near. It's a small block of flats, number thirty-one.'

She stared at him for a moment, her hands still trapping him there beneath her, and then she asked him: 'Why are you lying?'

'Lying? Why would I lie?' he said, feeling the lie coming apart.

'I don't know why you would lie,' she said, 'but I know there aren't any blocks of flats in South Yarra, small or otherwise.'

She continued to stare at him, her large amber eyes waiting for the answer, her body, too.

Perhaps he was so tired of running, so tired of lying, he had to tell someone, just to shift the yolk of it a little; perhaps there was something about her that made her the one to tell, liar to liar. He'd never know why, but he told her all right. 'You've got me,' he said. 'I don't live in South Yarra. I don't know Melbourne at all. I've come from Sydney, among other places. And I'm not going to Broome for any reason other than to leave the country. I'm in trouble with the police.'

'Oh,' she said, and she remained there, sitting on his hips, unfazed, unmoved but for the spark of interest that glittered in her tiger eyes, curious. 'Do tell.'

And so he did. She curled around him to listen, and over the next hour and more he told her every significant thing: growing up in the orphanage, son of a whore, sent on from there to the boys' home, then the industrial school, and then onto the navy, never getting higher than able seaman in rank; he told her about the beatings he'd endured in each of the institutions he'd known, he told her about his desperation to be free, to make something better of himself for whoever his mother might have been; he told her about jumping ship in New Zealand, mostly labouring on farms there, and making his way to Brisbane, mostly cutting cane, and then moving on to Sydney, where he finally talked his way into a decent job selling telephone sets for Lawrence & Hanson Electrical Company at Wynyard; he told her about the chance meeting with a certain real estate agent then, one night after work at the Square and Compass Hotel on George Street, not far from where he was boarding at the time: Fred McElroy, the estate agent who said he was looking for a sharp young fellow, a partner, a gentleman to sell house-and-land deals.

'Great deals for the working man to own his own beachside home,' Fin told her, and the bitterness in his words was hurled mostly at himself. 'Such an idiot, I was – I believed him. I knew it was too good to be true, I knew he was duping these buyers at Maroubra somehow, that things were not quite legitimate, but I never asked the questions I should have. I pocketed my wage from the business, and my cut of the commissions on each of the sales I'd made – and most of those sales *were* legitimate: some flats in Randwick, cottages around Watsons Bay, shops along Oxford Street at Paddington. I was making good money – but out at Maroubra, I was selling land that didn't exist, and in a big hurry. McElroy took the payments for the deposits in the office, and I never saw a penny of that lot. I suppose he thought that if anyone would get caught in the scam it would be me – the salesman, the man out front. I was his decoy.'

She didn't blench in the slightest at any word of all this; she didn't move from his side. So he told her the rest: 'McElroy never let me near the money, or the accounts generally, but that's obviously where the police needed to go to put a stop to it – and that's how they got him, taking a payment of cash, from a lure. I saw the whole thing, or heard it at least, from the side window of the office, in Bondi, just as I was coming back from showing a buyer a place in Bronte, grabbing a pie for lunch on the way. When they'd carted him out in handcuffs, I snuck back in through the window, grabbed what was in the petty cashbox in the desk, and I ran. And here I am. Not anyone called James Sinclair, either – for all that that's my registered name. The name my mother gave me is Finlay. My name is Finlay McFarland. This is who I really am.'

He felt her move then, but only closer, if that were possible.

'Finlay?' she said from under his arm, and he felt her voice in his ribs. 'That name is almost as fabulous as your story.' She shifted a little, to rest her chin upon her hand, upon his chest. 'Fin – hm. I like it. But I don't see why you need to leave the country. You need a good lawyer, that's all.'

Fin looked at her there beside him with a surge of every emotion he knew and a trace of something he'd never felt before. He'd never met anyone like her – not close up. He didn't know if he wanted to laugh or cry first; he said: 'A lawyer would be a good idea, yes, if I had any money for a good one, and if I had any desire to spend any time in prison.'

'You won't go to prison,' she said, and it sounded like a promise – one unlikely to be fulfilled.

'Irene.' He wasn't sure if she'd quite understood the gravity of his situation, so he distilled it to the bare facts. 'I've deserted from the Royal Navy, and I have facilitated a fraud, even if I wasn't fully aware of it at the time. I'll be going to prison for these things, if I'm caught. It's just a matter of how long I'd be asked to stay.'

'No, you won't be going anywhere near a prison,' she replied, sitting up as if she meant to take care of it straightaway. 'My very good friend in South Yarra is a chap by the name of E.M. Densforth the younger – aka my mate Marksy – aka son of Supreme Court Justice E.M. Densforth the elder, soon to take silk himself, and who will get you out of this without a whisper of a worry. He'll do it for fun – he'll do it for me.'

'What?' Now Fin did not quite understand; he couldn't conceive of such a gift; such a break. 'Why? Why would you …?'

'I don't know.' She grinned, so mischievously, and so convincingly. 'I suppose because I like you. I think I might like you rather a good deal, Finlay McFarland. And I happen to believe you, extraordinary as that may seem. I also believe you don't deserve the lot you've been tossed. I know some small thing of what it is to carry a weight, and so does Marksy. He'll help you sort it out – truly. He'll do anything for me – he's my fiancé.' She winked.

'And why would your fiancé …?' Fin understood less and less. Surely he was dreaming: this woman was unreal.

But her laughter was real enough. 'Because he's not my fiancé. He's not anyone's fiancé. He's a darling man, my Marksy, the best there is, and believe me, I would be tragically in love with him but he doesn't quite like girls the way a chap ought to. He'd prefer long months at sea, if you know what I mean. I'm his decoy. And he'll be absolutely indignant on your behalf at the treatment you've received. He will represent you as a matter of principle.'

'Ah.' Fin finally understood something of the situation here, and he might have laughed with her, but that he was remembering more of his own time at sea. Not everyone in the navy had been an arsehole: there was one warrant officer in particular, Geoff Rigby, who, being a nance himself, saw what was happening with Blackstone, and tried to help as best he could; for all that he hadn't been able to do much about it in the short term, it was Rigby's word that eventually got Fin put up a rank and transferred out to the *Psyche*. Men could be good to each other; men could act on principle alone. He'd needed the reminder of that; the hope of that, however slim it was. But still, he couldn't quite bring himself to wholly believe Irene here. He asked her: 'Why would you help me, really?'

'I don't know,' she said again, getting up to find a cigarette, telling him distractedly: 'Perhaps because I'm lost and motherless, too.'

He wasn't sure if that was a throwaway line; she couldn't seriously have been comparing her lot with his, could she? 'What happened to your mother?' he asked her, and the words fell out of his mouth, blunt and harsh.

'She …' Irene searched for her lighter, pulling her kimono around herself as she opened drawers and rummaged about the small chaotic world of her cabin, but he sensed she was searching for a way to avoid this turn in the conversation.

'I'm sorry,' he said quickly. 'It's not for me to know. I shouldn't have asked you that.'

'No, it's all right.' She found her lighter on the writing table, by her notebook there; she leant against the back of the chair, facing him, and lit her cigarette. 'Everyone knows,' she told the cigarette, 'even though no-one talks about it. When it happened, it unhappened at the same time. My father, my sisters, even Marg, who says what she likes, will never talk of it. It never happened.'

She looked at him now, briefly but plainly, so that he thought she might be inviting him to ask her about it, and so he did: 'What happened?'

'Mum. She ...' Irene drew the smoke deep into her lungs and exhaled it as she spoke. 'The doctor officially called it an accidental overdose of camphorated chlorodyne, taken for a bad tooth, but she left a note. I found it, on the bedside. *I am sorry, my beloved family, but I am so very exhausted. Please try to understand that I must sleep, and sleep.* There was no explanation other than that. No warning; no obvious depression. She drank two bottles of the tincture – she meant what she did. She meant to die. I found her, and the bottles. It was two days after my sister Oceanna's firstborn baby's first birthday, sweet, fat, little Rupert, we were all still gathered there, out at Everley, the station, and Mum had meant for us all to be there – she'd insisted I come all the way home for the party, miss the first few weeks of the university term for it, because it was almost my birthday, too. She was an inveterate nagger – a worrier.'

Irene paused to take another drag, and continued: 'Mum – she ... she'd always been quite nervy; neurotic, I suppose is the medical term; she never quite coped with the dust of Derby, the faint red smear over everything; or with the worry of Dad roaming around out on the boundaries, or with the heat – anywhere here in the west. The bigness of the spaces, the sky, I think they frightened her, wore her down ... Anyway, who knows why or what it was really all about? Only Mum could know that. It was seven years ago, just about precisely. I went back to university and unthought it all as well as I could. Life goes on, doesn't it? What else can one do but go on with it?'

'Right.' Fin nodded. 'I see.' There was her weight and her wound, no less painful than his.

And there, that day, that moment, as the *Koombana* gently rolled on through the waves, a pact was made between them, these lovers. The bond was fused. They barely knew it, but it was done.

*

He could only hear snatches of what they had said over the calls of the gulls that swooped and wheeled around the ship, but he had heard enough. Police Corporal Frank Buttle moved away from Miss Everley's window now, stepping back across the promenade to the rail, and stood there as if he might be enjoying the view of the coast as they neared it, the view over the flat, sandy expanse that was Geraldton.

Hedley Harris had warned him late last night that Miss Irene Everley might be heading for strife with this mysterious Sinclair bloke, and it seemed she was. As he leaned there on the rail he began to jot down all he had heard in his pocketbook, under the heading *March 13th*. What a pack of lies: an orphan's lament, hardship at an industrial school in Glasgow, rough time in the navy. This bloke had pulled every heart string there was, as if he was reading it from a script. He was good, too. It had sounded to Frank Buttle as if he'd even had Miss Everley denying she was engaged to that Melbourne barrister fellow – what was his name again? Densforth, that's right. Had her defences down so low she was revealing all about her poor mother into the bargain. What a tragic story that one was and too true – it had been Frank himself who'd taken the report from Doctor Fenton out at Everley Station, and arranged for the collection of the body for burial. Mrs Everley – sad, unfortunate Selena Everley – there'd always been something otherworldly about her, something distant, that way English-born women sometimes are. Not quite here.

He remembered young Miss Irene Everley's face that day – pale, as if her spirit had left, too. She'd made a joke that her mother had gone to great and terrible lengths to avoid her youngest daughter's attempt at making pancakes, and he'd fallen a little in love with the girl then, in a paternal sort of way – he was almost old enough to be her father. Her father – God forbid, what would Hal Everley do if he knew his youngest daughter was entertaining this strange bloke in her cabin? Frank knew what he himself would do if his own daughter, Marion, were in any similar situation. She was sixteen, preparing for her final school examinations in Perth with her own hopes of attending university in Adelaide, and he was already concerned about her leaving her mother.

At that thought, and not for the first time, his mind then turned to the possibility of moving his whole family to Adelaide, applying for a transfer, taking up a new posting with the South Australian Police Force. He knew that Minnie, his wife, would think it was a fine idea. After all, their son, Clement, was already at university there, doing well at engineering. He made a mental note to look into it with a serious view now, see what might be on offer, have them all settled across the state line next year. Perhaps even seek a promotion – and he was bloody well due one of those.

He was getting ahead of himself here, though, and returned to his note-taking on this Sinclair-McFarland puzzle. He was sure he'd seen a national alert in one of the recent police gazettes, perhaps in the *West Australian* newspaper, that a real estate swindler by the name of Mc something or other was on the run from Sydney; that name Maroubra seemed to ring a bell, too. He'd only had half an eye on the news, though, as Minnie had badgered him about never taking his holidays properly, never quite relaxing with the family. But his police mind switched into sharp focus here today: something else for him to look into. *Send telegram to WA Commissioner's office, confirm details/description of fraud from NSW*, he wrote. I think I might just have our man, he thought – they had to be one and the same, didn't they? It was too much of a coincidence for it to be otherwise.

Most opportune for himself, too, he realised, his mind drawn yet again by that promotion he so desired and believed he was entitled to. He imagined himself arresting the bloke, arranging the interstate prisoner transport, signing the extradition warrant –

finally winning some respect for his efforts, too. And at this his resentment flared.

Nineteen years he'd given to the Western Australian Police, taken all the remote and lonely postings, too, and although his family had done reasonably well by it, they had suffered his absences. Minnie worried particularly about the natives, the conflict that continued in the frontier country of the Kimberley, the attacks on the sparsely manned stations, like Everley. The Aborigines out there had no fear of the law, or of gaol. They had their spears and their dogs and they took whatever they wanted. One of Hal Everley's stock managers, his son-in-law Derek Brand, would tell a lively tale about being surrounded out there by more than a hundred one time, pulling out his harmonica and getting them all dancing a jig to break the mood of war – bullshit of course. Frank Buttle knew that there's only one way out of a situation such as that: with a rifle. Hal Everley was right: the natives should be given their own land. But smart as Hal might have been, that was never going to happen, not in Western Australia, where most would rather lose a hundred head of cattle than give the black man an inch.

Or give an Anglican police corporal a crack at a promotion in the Roman Catholic stronghold that was the West Australian Force. Yes, Frank Buttle thought as he leaned there on the rail looking out at the desolate, wind-beaten coast: if he could catch this crook McFarland, or whoever he was, and rescue Irene Everley in one hand, he'd have himself that Adelaide posting, and maybe command of a suburban station, to see out his next nineteen years – as sergeant.

As the ship now edged into Champion Bay, Frank Buttle moved off down the promenade. He'd send that telegram to the West Australian Police Commissioner's office out of Geraldton today. He'd have his future prospects all nicely lined up before this journey was finished. He'd have the bloke in cuffs before they reached Broome; he'd have him before the Nor'-West magistrate when they docked there.

MIYA

Koombana is a word that means peace, in the language of the people of the far south-west. It was a fashion of the Adelaide Steamship Company to give their vessels these kinds of native names – the SS *Yongala* had been so named for a word of the central desert people meaning beautiful water; the SS *Bullarra* was named for a word meaning rainbow in one language and the joyful water spout of the whale in another. A strange custom, it seemed to me, as the only native black man I would ever see on board such a ship was in chains.

A boy such as Warlitj, the boy who found me and brought me into the air, could not even get anywhere near an Adelaide Steamship Company vessel at the wharf. That didn't stop him from coming into town on the days these big ships came in, though; it was something to do, and he was always hopeful some work might come his way, as it occasionally did, shovelling manure from the waterside pens or lugging bags of grain onto drays. On this day, though, he'd come running back into town when he'd heard the wildfire shouts of horror that spread out across Port Hedland on the discovery of the bloodied corpses of Jock Matheson and Lucky Zhang Yong. And he had known immediately that it had had something to do with me – according to the law as he knew it and felt it, the spirits were in chaos and would not rest until I was returned to where I belonged: into the sea, or into the wisdom of his grandfather.

There was nothing Warlitj could do now, though, except watch. He did not know that I was clutched tight in the hand of Han Wang

Chao, there in the back of the shell-packing shed, and there when the police found the Chinaman hiding, dragging him up by the elbows and throwing him into the lock-up. Warlitj watched as he was led away and he wanted to tell the policemen that things weren't exactly what they seemed, but he knew no-one would believe him, he knew he would make no sense to them, he knew he would most likely only be thrown into the lock-up, too, and so he stayed silent.

He ran home again, to the backwater scrub of Stingray Creek, and finally summoned the courage to tell his grandfather all that had happened, but when he did his grandfather only shook his tired, old head, and told Warlitj that he was the one who was in chaos. The old man told him it was time for him to go into the desert, to his mother's people, for he didn't believe the boy, either. A big pink pearl? A powerful, singing pearl? He thought his grandson was going mad with boredom, living too close to town, too many strange ideas from the white devils mixing things up in his head, his imagination getting away with him. The boy needed to become a man; he needed his cousins to show him, take him through all the right ceremonies, so he would know the real spirits. Warlitj did not agree: he was frightened of those desert cousins – all of them hunters – but he could only obey.

Han Wang Chao could only sit and stare in the cell at Port Hedland police station, while he awaited his removal to Broome, for trial. It took several days, and all the while he clutched me in his hand. His thoughts had become quiet around the certainty that all would be well so long as he held me; his mind was empty but for that belief. He did not even seem to understand his predicament when the prosecutor came to him and explained that in all likelihood he would be hanged.

It was not until the trial itself in Broome that I was discovered. One of the witness statements taken from the various patrons of the Pier Hotel made mention that Matheson had boasted of finding a sixty-grain rose-tinted pearl before he was murdered, and the case for the prosecution then picked out this detail as the motive for Han Wang Chao's gruesome spree.

'And where is this pearl?' the magistrate asked the prosecutor, who could only shrug in response and mumble something about

Matheson having been a renowned liar and braggart, when in actuality, all involved had been too quick to see the worthless Chinaman dispatched and executed to bother with the finer points of their system of laws, such as evidence. As for the defence, Han Wang Chao's barrister was barely able to commit his client's name to memory, much less have garnered any useful information about motive. The incompetence and blind bigotry of the whole case was initially astonishing to me, considering these people otherwise professed and demanded such faith in their rules and regulations, imposing them upon all others as superior throughout the entirety of the human world.

But the magistrate, Justice Barrington Marbelow, was not at all surprised; nor was he interested much in the notion of justice. He ordered his clerk, Jake Bevin, to search the prisoner personally at the next recess, and instructed: 'If you find anything on him, bring it directly to me.'

It was at that moment that I began to sing to Barrington Marbelow. I caught the trace of lust that had flashed through him at the thought of a sixty-grain pink, and I told him: *If I exist, I am yours.* I knew then that there was little chance I could convince him to return me to the sea, but at that time he was the only one among this tribe of fools who could hear me at all – my only chance at anything other than remaining clasped in the hand of a dead man or dropped into the sawdust below the hangman's trapdoor.

Jake Bevin did his master's bidding, searching every pocket and seam of the prisoner's clothes, searching inside his mouth and even between his toes, before finally prising me from Han's desperate fist as the court warden held him with an arm round his neck, near choking him until he fell unconscious.

'What is it?' the court warden asked as Jake Bevin left the cell, with me now held tight in his own fist.

'Nothing of interest to you,' was the abrupt and dismissive reply.

It would have been his reply to Barrington Marbelow, too, if he had not been so intimidated by the man, his arrogance and indifference, the bold corruptions of his authority. Jake Bevin began to open his mind to me himself then. I saw that he had debts to pay, his clerk's salary never covering his expenses, his own family, wheat farmers in Esperance, struggling themselves, too stretched to ever help. What Jake wouldn't give to be able to afford to undertake a degree in the law himself – to win a scholarship, or find a benefactor.

He would find none in Marbelow.

'Did you find anything on him?' the magistrate asked over his luncheon tray of roast chicken and chilled Chablis.

'I did.' Jake Bevin, against his own desires, placed me on the deep-green leather inlay of Marbelow's desk.

'Christ Almighty, look at that.' Marbelow peered at me, and then he said to his clerk: 'Damned bugger will be hanged for a worthless ball of paste – that's the most preposterous fake I've ever seen.'

'Fake, sir?' Jake had thought I had felt real in his hand – cool and heavy, as genuine pearls are.

'Fake, yes,' said Marbelow. 'Now leave me to my lunch.'

Jake heard him open the desk drawer as he left; he heard the key turn, too. He knew. Oh yes, he knew: I was no fake.

And I had been stolen again.

And again, I would have my revenge.

IRENE

'We missed you at lunch?' Suzette smiles daggers at me as I settle into the club chair by hers at the card table. I might have found any number of excuses to break this saloon euchre date I so impetuously and incredibly suggested this morning, but it's some atonement for all my sins, I suppose; some pain for all the pleasure I have enjoyed thus far today.

'Hm,' I sigh, boring myself with the repetition of the excuse. 'This interminable damp, hot yuck has had me utterly vaporised. I am a cloud.' I glance out of the window behind her, out to sea, and the entire sky is a thin and sticky cloud. The heat slows time; I want supper to roll round again as quickly as possible, so that I might dispense with time altogether for a while: look only into his face, decide if his eyes are green or grey or brown, and not decide anything at all as he tells me more. His story whorls around me like smoke. Do I really believe him? There seems no reason not to; and even if he's only spun me a load of lies, I have to know why. I have to know why he is unravelling all of mine.

Suzette leans towards me as though merely pushing the deck of cards my way. 'We know what you've been up to,' she whispers, so that the Skamp sisters cannot hear across the table. 'Ennis has seen his comings and goings from your cabin.'

'Ennis who and what?' I slice her in half with my next glance, but my pulse leaps over my smile, which tells her: your maid is a nasty little bitch then, just like you, isn't she. Suzette's cabin is up the other end of the corridor and round the corner – effort has gone into this pitiful little ploy.

'I can understand the attraction. He's very handsome, this Mr Sinclair – that's his name, isn't it? I feel so sorry for Edward, though ...' Suzette returns my smile and it's so thin, she's so thin, she is a starving, desperate bitch who thinks she's just snatched a lamb. I glance again at Alice and Gennie Skamp, but they remain deep in some conversation of their own.

'You don't know what you're talking about,' I hiss at Suzette, my venom undisguised.

'Don't I?' She smiles ever more thinly, as the steward brings the coffee pot. 'It seems everyone is having a wild romance. Even my cousin Beatrice – you remember Beatrice, from university days. Bespectacled? Bookish? Well, well, love has taken her to Melbourne, where she's entangled as we speak in a mad-passionate with Phil Oswald – you know, the editor from *Australian Life Weekly*? It's an outrage, and extremely hush-oh. So is all I've heard via that channel about your *career*.'

So that is her trump over me? I might gasp at it – not least at the thought of Phil being passionate about anything apart from the printing date for the paper – but the urge to groan overruns this breath. I don't really recall Beatrice, no, but the incestuousness of this tiny-minded country is impossible to forget, much less avoid. No wonder I give myself to strangers and their strange tales.

I guess at her ulterior intentions, and tell her: 'If you think anything you believe you know might in any way drive *Edward* and I apart, think again. You really have no idea about Marksy and me.'

She shrugs with confected innocence and I almost feel embarrassed for her, even before she says: 'If Wynne and I weren't so in love, I might be frightfully jealous.'

Because she is frightfully jealous; I don't think she knows how to be any other way. I feel so sorry for Wynne. I look away, lean across the edge of the table to Alice at my left, my mind reeling around only one thing, only one essential repetition: protecting Dad from all of this; from me. That's all that matters: my father's heart. But how will I protect him? There is only one way: tell him the truth, and be the only one to tell him – as soon as I am home. *Daddy, I want to be a writer. I want to be a truth-teller. I don't want to be anything else. And so I have to leave; I'm so very sorry, but I have to go. For the best, for everyone.*

I ask Alice Skamp now: 'Swap seats?' So that she might pair with her sister, and I might keep Suzette Leighton where I can most effectively trump her in return. 'Shall we summon the cake trolley, too?'

'Oh what a good idea.' Alice smiles back at me, and just as she stands, just as she turns to catch the eye of the cake-trolley steward, I catch the look of sympathy in her eye. I'm not sure what the look means – sympathy that I have so willingly volunteered to endure Suzette Leighton for my euchre pair, or sympathy that my secrets are on the out, I don't know, and I don't much care.

As I stand again, I look over my shoulder, and see Mr Davis with Marg out there on the promenade looking towards Geraldton, last post of civilisation before the topics that it is. He's pointing at something on the dock; she laughs at whatever he says. She's forgotten all about me today. A seagull perches on the rail beside them, listening in; the shallows spangle, the pale turquoise tinselled before them under the high sun. And there is something of my pleasure restored.

'My deal, ladies.' I grab up the cards as I take my chair, opposite my pair, grinning at her. 'Suzette – you score.'

And I laugh at her face: she can't add up. Missed the intelligence trolley the day brains were being handed out, this one. I shall see to it that she won't take a trick all afternoon, either. Oh how I love to lose – for a good cause.

FIN

He knew he had fallen hard and fast for her, and it was more than inconvenient. She intensified every longing he knew: his deepest need to simply be, to simply love and be loved. No other woman drew him to her as she did.

It was only because she was so very beautiful, he told himself as he strode, head down, hands in pockets, across the busy dock; it was only because she was so free to do as she pleased; because she was so very unattainable. This was a shipboard fling; an illusion. She would soon forget her promises to help him, as soon as she stepped back onto dry land. If he allowed himself to get too wrapped up in her, he would only end up precisely where he least wanted to be: prison. Her fiancé who wasn't her fiancé was a barrister, was he? It was all too good to be true – too ridiculous. What could a barrister in Melbourne do for him here, anyway? Likely nothing – and double that if he was caught. He would be tried in New South Wales, not in Victoria, not in Western Australia; he'd be cuffed and chained and shipped back on the next mail east, addressed to Darlinghurst Gaol, Sydney. She might have hoped she could help him, she might have meant what she said, but it simply wasn't realistic. It wasn't going to happen.

He kept on into the town of Geraldton, a startling strip of wealth rising up from dust that was the colour of porridge and stunted scrub that looked as though it didn't want to be here, either. It was a town made rich from lead and copper mines, and the cattle trade – so he'd read in that copy of *Western Australia: The Past and the Future*. There was gold lettering on every awning and shopfront he walked by, and in every glint he saw her eyes: her bright and haunted eyes. Wanting.

His collar felt as if it were tightening around his neck and he loosened his tie a little as he continued towards the first tobacconist he saw. He was looking for a newspaper, for the shipping schedule – looking for his escape route.

'There's the *Guardian* there,' the man at the counter said. 'Fresh off the press this morning.'

Fin handed over a penny for it, and he stood there in the shop to read what he needed to, finding it on the front page: another ship for Broome would be here in eleven days, leaving from this port and going on to the Malaccas; the one he was on, the *Koombana*, would be going on to Wyndham for the Tanami Goldfields and then the port of Darwin, where he now saw he could pick up a mail going to the East Indies, or one to Singapore a few days later from Broome. All the other ships here were schooners and similar smaller vessels, not leaving the waters of this continent. He looked back out the door of the shop, towards the docks, as if some other option might appear. But all he could see was a mob of cattle moving down the street, like a line of passengers.

'You're from the ship, aren't you?' A man beside him asked.

Fin turned to look at him: a man about the same height as himself, very pale and clear blue eyes, thin moustache precisely kept, hair cropped close and greying at the temples.

'Buttle.' The man extended his hand. 'Frank Buttle – corporal of police, Derby.'

'Jim Sinclair.' Fin took the shake firmly, and he didn't blink, for all that he immediately feared. He smiled with all his charm. 'Lieutenant of Royal Navy – prematurely retired.'

'Pleased to make your acquaintance,' the policeman said, and he didn't smile as he looked at Fin, regarding him intently with that clear and piercing stare.

He's onto me, Fin thought, but dismissed it as quickly, before the shake was done. He was only jumping at shadows where there were none, he told himself. He told this Buttle: 'Pleased, I'm sure

I am, too.' Then he looked away out the door once more, as if preoccupied by some pleasant thing, adding vaguely: 'Time to be back on board, I suppose. No doubt we'll meet again there.'

'Yes, we will,' Buttle replied and he held that stare of his as Fin turned to leave.

Fin felt it burning into his back, out into the street. He felt the bars of his cage closing in on him, but he told himself, haven't I always felt that? He had never known life without fear of a trap.

What difference would it make to wait here for the ship going on to the Malaccas or return to the *Koombana*, press on for Broome, stay with the original plan, such as it was? The difference was Irene Everley, and he could not resist. If he was doomed, let him be doomed for her, for the handful of days they had left.

As he met the gangway of the ship once more, he looked down at the slice of green harbour between dock and hull and he wondered within a heartbeat what it might be like to slip into the sea. Slip away permanently. *I must sleep, and sleep*, Irene's mother had written, and he knew that thought himself, that desire, that weariness – he had looked down from that edge many times – but he dismissed it now, too, as he always had, for another shadow that wasn't really there. Why would he end his life when he had yet to win the fight for that life to truly begin?

Once aboard, he made his way aft of the dining room on the spar deck, intending to take the crew's companionway up from there. He would avoid the first-class social halls for the moment, on his way back to his cabin, to dress for dinner. Sense and survival insisted he lock himself in that cabin when he got there, and stay there, but he wanted to see her across the dining table, he wanted to pretend he might court her; he wanted to pretend she was his. If this was all he could have, why not? His mind flipped one way and then the other, like a fish thrashing about for air.

The air was almost liquid here, though, with the warmth of the boilers rising up through the centre of the ship. He could feel the rush of fire and steam below as memories etched upon his bones, so that he thought he might have been imagining it when her name seemed to fall across his path, out of the open laundry-room door.

'That Miss Everley is ...'

He stopped in his stride, took a step back to wonder if that's what he'd really just heard, and as he did he saw two stewardesses and what appeared to be a lady's maid at their work, folding, ironing. He stayed there, just out of sight, watching through the crack between door and frame, listening to their conversation.

'My Mrs Leighton doesn't think much of her, and I don't either. She's sleeping with that tasty-looking Mr Sinclair from number eleven – how is that for sluttish? One rule for some, hm? Mrs Leighton says he's not even of their circle – he's just some come-along stranger.'

That's it, Fin thought at this: here is a warning that might as well have been written on the air in solid steel, telling him to leave Irene Everley alone.

The two stewardesses stopped their folding and ironing, and for a moment they stood there in the silence of their own amazement, until the older of the pair, a sturdy woman of middle age, said to the maid: 'I'll not have that language in my laundry, thank you, Ennis Priestly – or anywhere on this ship. And I'll have you know that Miss Everley has always been kind to me and all who serve her. I do not believe for a moment that a lady like her would do such a dreadful thing. You take that terrible tongue of yours and make it still.'

'I'm sorry, Mrs Freer.' The maid hung her head a little, but without any shame she went on: 'I can only say what I saw – and heard. They weren't dancing in there, I don't think. Well, not standing upright, at any rate. Unless they were dancing on the bedsprings. In the middle of the day!'

'Oh, Ennis, you wicked thing! How can you even speak those words aloud!' the younger of the stewardesses exclaimed, her voice sky high and Irish, coarse with laughter.

Until she was promptly remonstrated by the older woman, too. 'Delia! You will stop this footling and gassing about and get on with your work. And you listen to me – listen to me very carefully, my girl – if you repeat any of these lies, you will be without any work at all, do you hear me? And you won't be making any more sneaky visits to see your Bill Burkin in the night, either. Don't you think for a moment that I don't know what *you* do when I'm not looking. I could easily let Chief Steward know about all that and you'll be put off at Port of Denham. Is that clear?'

'Yes, Mrs Freer,' the younger woman replied; she hung her head in fear of that consequence.

And Fin went on his way then, smiling at recognising the voice of the older woman here: that woman from last night, getting into the cook about his filthy saucepans. This was obviously her ship. And Irene Everley was surely someone special to be defended by her. Defended by one who served her. Is there any greater proof of honour or substance than this?

Irene Everley. She was as real as she was beautiful, and he was more drawn to her with every step he took now – every breath.

MIYA

Han Wang Chao was found hanged in his cell three days later, before the sentence was read, but whether that was by his own choice or by the force of others I did not know, although I suspected it was the latter. I remained in the desk drawer of Justice Barrington Marbelow all that while – and he would be dead soon, too, that same afternoon.

From the moment he claimed me as his own, this magistrate sought only to profit. The mind of Marbelow was serpentine, ceaselessly crawling with calculations. First, he had given me a new and more distinguished name – the Roseate Pearl – and then he had begun to invent a more saleable provenance for me, noting in his journal, as if it were fact, that I had been purchased from a Japanese who was so knocked about in the brain from diving he didn't know what a small treasure he'd held in his hand when he sold me to Marbelow for £500 at the bar of the Roebuck Bay Hotel. Marbelow even had me valued by a Dutch dealer who happened to be in town at that time. The dealer, Dirk van Gossen, offered him £3000 immediately: the Dutchman had never seen a pearl so large and so deeply tinged. But Marbelow, once he saw the dealer's eyes light up with his own greed, thought he might do better than that – he thought then that he might sell me for nearer £5000 to an old associate in Delhi, who'd had past dealings with the antiquary and jewel buyer for the Maharaja of Jaipur.

Why did Marbelow do any of this? Why did he steal me at all? It wasn't as though he needed the money. His home on the bay in Broome was lavish in every way, seat of the greatest refinement in the Kimberley, no lower-class nouveau riche, no Irish, no Papists, no Jews allowed. He considered himself to be the primary arbiter of taste and gentility in the entire region, and most deferred to him as such. He owned substantial tracts of pastoral land in the Nor'-West and in the Territory, a parcel of which from the latter had been found to contain such a quantity of gold that his sons and his grandsons and his great-grandsons would never know anything but wealth. He even possessed a wife who, after thirty-two years wedded to his disregard, found reasons to continue to be utterly devoted to him. He had no reason to steal me other than that he saw he could, and believed he should possess me, so that he might sell me to the highest bidder, sell me to an Indian prince, merely to gratify his own conceit. A convoluted plot devised to satisfy himself of his own genius.

I could have taunted him somehow, perhaps, attempted to bring him down, to have him see himself for what he really was, but what I sensed of his soul prevented me: there appeared to be nothing there. Marbelow, it seemed, couldn't even hear me. It took me those three days in his possession to locate his spirit at all, and I only did when he sent out a faint streak of relief upon the receipt of the news that Han Wang Chao was dead, and with that any hard evidence of what Marbelow himself had done.

He had no other thought or feeling for the Chinese, only contempt. 'Leave now,' he dismissed the police constable who had reported the premature hanging to him, and then he returned to the correspondence he had been attending to before the interruption. It was a letter from a judicial colleague in Perth, from the Aborigines' Protection Department, requesting his advice on the number of suspicious cases of accidental poisoning of Aborigines in the East Kimberley – so many native women mistaking arsenic for baking powder? Surely there needed to be some coronial investigation, the colleague enquired. Before Marbelow began to compose his response, before he looked up at his clerk who waited there to take its dictation, the images of two children flickered through his mind:

small, brown-skinned, blond curls, hiding behind their mother's skirts: his own children, a girl and a boy, by a housemaid. He had had the children sent to a reserve, on an island far away; that was the Christian thing to do. But if he could express himself frankly on the matter, he would advise the department that all Aborigines should be drowned at birth.

At that moment, I sent out such a scream I felt it as a crashing, splintering of shell, of stone; it penetrated through his bones. My scream reached deep into his flesh and sought out his beating heart, then stopped it as a fist might crush the life from a scrambling rat. At first I did not comprehend what had occurred; what I had done: that I had become not merely the agent of destruction, but a destroyer myself. All I could feel was the deeper pulsing of my light, an engorgement and expansion of my being that was thrilling and daunting at once – a tiny glimmer of my power to come.

For now though, there in Marbelow's chambers, Jake Bevin, the clerk, panicked and sprang around the desk to his master, tearing at his shirt collar, and trying to shake him back to life. But it was clear that the magistrate was gone. He was dead.

Jake Bevin was seized by dread then, layers of it rising up around him – he was terrified most of all that he had just lost his employment with the death of Justice Marbelow; terrified, too, that he might be somehow blamed for the calamity that had occurred here – and so I began singing immediately to him, singing into his confusion.

Open the drawer and find me there, I commanded him. *Take the pearl. Take me for yourself, and all of your worries will disappear.*

When he heard me, when my voice first filled his mind with what he took for inspiration, Jake did not hesitate. The key was already in the lock; all he had to do was turn it, and he did. And there I was: rolling between Marbelow's letter opener and a tin of peppermints.

Take me to the sea, I urged Jake Bevin. *Take me deep into the water*, I demanded with all the force of my desire to be returned, hoping that, as much as my ability to kill had increased, so had the power of my song. But Jake either did not hear this last command, or he ignored it.

He picked me up between thumb and forefinger, and I felt his relief, a steadying of his nerves. 'You Big Pink Wonder,' he called me before he put me in the fob pocket of his waistcoat. All he could see or hear now was the payment of his debts, and his resentment of his poverty.

I was not unsympathetic, not at all. The life of such a low-ranked public servant was one bound by constant frustration: always required to keep up appearances, but never quite being able to comfortably afford to; always having ambition dangled before you as a golden carrot, but never quite having the means to reach it. And it was not cheap living in the Nor'-West, where everything from a bunch of bananas to a pot of boot polish was twice the price as elsewhere. Which all explained why he owed just over twenty pounds in scant bits and pieces to the publican at the Star Hotel, a sum comprised of rent arrears and losses at cards and billiards – small flutters he'd indulge in after a claret but always in the attempt, in the hope, of getting ahead.

Who wouldn't pity him? But pity was not relevant to my needs, not relevant to the laws of nature that drove my will.

Later that night, after the doctor, the police and the undertaker had come and gone, carrying Marbelow away by mortuary hearse, Jake Bevin retired to the Star, where he boarded. With his mind lurching between what he would do with me and the shock of his master's sudden demise, he ordered a bottle of claret from the bar, intending to take it directly to his room. But there at the bar he found himself standing right by a dealer he knew – Mark Liebglid. Everyone knew Liebglid: he was well liked and was almost as well known as the town's other prominent Jews, Davis and Rubin, but he was not as wealthy, and he had no British connections; he was Polish, and there was always a whisper about him that, in the underworld of Broome's ever-vibrant economy, Liebglid was not averse to smuggling a little snide – that is, trading in stolen pearls.

Jake Bevin couldn't believe the way his fortunes had run today. First, his master had dropped stone-cold dead in front of him, virtually tossing this enormous and unusual pearl into his hand, and now the perfect dealer had appeared as if by some mystical design to take it off his conscience less than four hours later. Would that there had been a design at work here, beyond blind luck.

'Liebglid,' Bevin turned to him at the bar. 'You are just the man I need to see. I have something interesting to show you – in private.'

And in the privacy of his room upstairs at the hotel, Jake Bevin showed Mark Liebglid his prize.

'Big Pink Wonder, I'll say.' Liebglid whistled as he held me up to the lamp, and he knew what he was looking at. A few days earlier, he'd had a drink with Dirk van Gossen at the Roebuck, who'd told him of me. Dirk did not say who had shown me to him, but he'd said he'd suspected the large rose-coloured pearl was snide and to be careful of it – that there was something strange about the story behind it, something that didn't quite add up. All Liebglid could think of, as I began to sing to him, too, was: £3000, that's what Dirk had offered, but he'd said it would probably sell for much more.

Much more, I sang to Liebglid. *Take me down to the docks, take me down to the water.*

Liebglid told Bevin: 'I will give you three hundred and fifty – and I don't want to know where you got it. All right?'

Three hundred and fifty pounds was a fortune as far as Jake Bevin was concerned; it was the answer to all his problems; it was his future secured, for the time being at least. 'Done,' he said, and they shook on it.

I regretted that pity or sympathy could not have saved Jake Bevin now, but that he had in actuality secured his future. He drank the rest of that bottle of claret alone; he returned downstairs and paid the publican what he owed. He then left the hotel and walked out into the sea. I would discover some days later that he had drowned, his body washed into the mouth of Dampier Creek. Why did he do this? I don't know. Perhaps he was tormented by some echo of my song, compelling him into the deep water; perhaps his problems were far larger than I knew. I couldn't sense his reasoning, or lack of it. I was not with his mind at the time he chose to do it. By then I was too far from him, at least in my own concerns. I was on my way to another beach, further along the western stretch of Roebuck Bay, with Liebglid – and he wouldn't fare much better.

IRENE

Lo! And on the sixth day, he moves through the dining room towards me as if there is no-one else here, nothing in the way of us but a couple of palm fronds and a ceiling pillar, which he smiles around as he finds me at the table; one hand in his pocket, sometimes the left, sometimes the right – the left tonight – and the slightest of salutes with the other, redefining suave as he goes. No-one knows his cares; no-one would guess at how completely he recreates my world – I can scarcely believe it myself. This perfect animal. With every day I am deeper in want of him, heavier and heavier in the hips for him, and yet so full of light I am carrying a small sun inside me. A small universe. I am so open, as I have never been – fabulously, irreparably broken open.

'Miss Everley?' Mr Davis is holding the bottle of wine over my glass, about to pour.

'Oh, no thank you – not tonight.' I'm busy for the moment anticipating the jump and quiver of every reflex that occurs whenever Fin takes his seat beside mine. Ah – and here he is; the edge of his sleeve cuff just touching against the top of my thigh, through the fabric of my gown. It's some kind of chemical reaction; an effervescence whispering all over my skin.

'Again?' Mr Davis is amused and curious – by my persistent sobriety on this voyage. 'No wine?'

'No.' I make a face, pretending disdain; he makes one pretending disapproval, but he approves; he gives Fin a congenial, 'Good evening,

Mr Sinclair,' with the sweetest trace of a warning that he is being observed, although dear Mr Davis hasn't seen the half of it, and never will. Blood rushes to my cheeks; fills my breasts: I never want my senses dulled again.

Finlay McFarland brushes a knuckle over the back of my hand, beneath the tablecloth, and I want him for my supper every night. I will have him. Again and again I leap over each of the obstacles in my mind: Marksy will deal with the legalities, of course he will; and Dad will be overjoyed – after he recovers from the initial confusion and dismay. Perhaps. Dad might be an uncouth bushwhacker from the Kimberley via the backblocks of the Kentish coast, whose greatest philosophical leap has been to switch from dairy to beef, he might be a little dense indeed, but he has never broken a law; never bent a rule. He's going to be more than a little dismayed. *I'm* a little dismayed: what exactly am I contemplating doing here? I have no intention of tethering myself to any man; no, I do not. And yet the idea of spending a day apart from this one has become unthinkable. Isn't life strange? So wonderfully strange. I am drunk enough on it alone.

A freak wave now tips the whole thing sideways and the butter dish slides across the tablecloth, Fin's hand quick to catch it before it falls to the floor, and I start laughing like a drain. I am laughing at his perfect hand: the night before last he told me of the man called Blackstone who smashed both of them with a crowbar; I want to smash all wrong things to avenge his suffering. I will smash all wrongness with my pencil. One day. I laugh louder again at that, because this desire in me has never been more of a dare, nor more essential. I want everything – with sauce.

'Honestly, Tigs.' Marg rolls her eyes, but she's not chiding me too sharply. She is fondling the stem of her glass, opposite me; I'm not sure that she even felt the ship roll, because she's enjoying the wonders of her own unfolding too much. Honestly. When I had sent out my vague wishes for some affection to blossom between her and Mr Davis, I'd sent them at least half selfishly, to have her well taken care of before I move on, and the other half not very seriously, given their significant differences in both age and religion, but it seems the universe heard and decided to do something like the right thing for them, too – minus the insane, oak-splitting sex, I can only presume. They've been promenade-strolling every day, deep in conversation; she even accompanied him and his assistant by lighter out into Shark Bay, where he showed her what he looks for in a raw, unmade pearl when he's on the hunt amongst the dealers there. And yesterday, in Onslow, looking for something for Dorothy, his daughter, they found not Pilbara rubies, but a hunk of amethyst, with a rich twist of indigo within it that Marg says looks like the spirit of all dance caught in crystal. At Marg's suggestion, he'll have it made into a princess-length double-strander – so very grown up, but not too grown up. Mr Davis smiles at her smiling at me now and I can only start laughing again – and more. What's this? I am happy; stupidly happy. I don't remember ever feeling so happy.

My laughter causes Fin to laugh, too. He is slow to laugh, but when he does, the cool, quiet baritone of its melody slides down the back of my neck, down my spine. And I have to laugh just a bit more now so that I don't scream.

'What a merry foursome you all make.' Suzette appears on the other side of me, at my shoulder, pin ever ready to prick balloons. 'May we join you here tonight?'

'Of course.' Mr Davis is quick to stand. 'Mrs Leighton, Miss Skamp and Miss Skamp. Join us, join us, please do.'

Oh look, and it's the Chief Wet Sock of Derby, Corporal Buttle, with them. Please don't join us: there's something about that man I have an aversion to, and not only because he's a policeman who knows my father; I don't want him near me, even if I'm not entirely sure why. I can hardly object to him joining us, though – or Suzette, or anyone, for that matter. Why would I? Happy people don't object to others sitting down to dinner wherever they so choose.

I smile into the palm fronds, and fan my face with my menu, a little dizzy from all that hysteria just now, and the persistent heat. God, it's been unrelentingly hot. So stubbornly hot, hotter and hotter, and yet the men at my table – all three of them – are such determined gentlemen, each for their own desperate reasons, none of them will take off their dinner jackets – or at least no-one wants to be the first to crack. My skin has gone from effervescent to sticky prickling just looking at them.

'Oh please, Mr Sinclair,' I tell the table, as I continue to fan my face. 'Do take off your jacket. Please – all of you.'

They do as they are told; I watch Fin place his jacket on the back of his chair. Mr Sinclair. How I have loved this subterfuge, calling him by that name in company, as though I play a part in some scheme of international espionage. But is that all I am doing here? The question suddenly rings through me. Am I merely romancing myself? My universe shifts and twists with eerie anxiety, a cold threat, inside me. Perhaps I am ill. Perhaps I've been ill all week, since leaving Perth. The humidity has seeped into my brain. I am going mad; perhaps as Mum did. In all this heat. Too much space; too little to do inside it. Perhaps there's a streak of self-annihilation that runs through the female line and I am the inheritor. I possess all of my father's recklessness and all of my mother's.

'You are closer and closer each time I see you.' Suzette slithers in beside me, her voice low and just for me.

'Even with our chairs fixed to the floor?' I bat her pettiness back at her with some other reflex, one that returns me to the earth, to my senses.

'Yes.' She purses her witchy little lips that way she does and she says: 'Wynne will be almost as devastated as Edward when they all find out, they are so like brothers.'

They are not. They are old school mates and erstwhile lovers of a good deal more than just rugby. But even as she continues to jab at me with her nastiness, I won't tell her this. I wouldn't betray them; but I also couldn't be that much of a pathological bitch.

'Suzy,' I ask her, genuinely enquiring, and also reaffirming to myself. 'What's to be devastated about? A man and a woman can have a friendship, you know. Me, Marksy, Mr Sinclair – friends above all else.'

I leave that there between us for her to puzzle over, but before she looks away I catch a glimpse of her devastation, perhaps; a look that reveals what I have guessed anyway: she has no friendship with her husband. She has no happiness with Wynne. Is she a friend of anyone's? Suzette Leighton has begun to break my heart. Strangest of all, this hits me in the pit. I could cry for her. I am so broken open I could cry for every friendless soul. More proof that I am, indeed, right off my sweet onion.

'London?' Mr Davis is conversing with Corporal Buttle, around Marg, who sits between them, and I follow his thoughts to get away from my own. 'No, I am not sure that I will ever return there, mild summers or not.'

'Oh? Why's that?' Chief Wet Sock asks; or rather, interrogates. He might be a dull chap, and certainly handsome in all the correct ways, but his penetrating gaze is disconcerting – startling. Makes one feel guilty for breathing. 'You do most of your business in London, don't you?' he asks Mr Davis as if it would be a crime not to. 'Isn't your partner, Mr Rubin, established there now?'

'Yes, but that world is a cold, old world,' Mr Davis answers, almost wistfully, talking to himself, regret returning to his words. 'I don't need to know it any more than I already do. Everything is about money there – everything – even while they pretend it is all about class, about tradition, history. At least in America they don't lie about it, but in London, in fact in all of Europe, they are like chess pieces stuck on the board, stuck in their squares. Stuck there by money, money, money. Look at Britain and Germany, France, too, empires squinting at each other like greedy and resentful old men, squabbling over shipping lanes and trading rights. They will break out in war soon if they can't work out fair dealings between themselves.'

'War? Surely not.' The corporal is nonplussed; ever hard to discern if he's a little slow or just deliberate in that constabulary way. 'But Europe is so much more progressed in civilisation than anywhere else in the world – London especially. What would be the point of the turmoil of war for them, for business?'

Mr Davis laughs now, sardonically, and Fin leans a little forward to listen to his answer. 'War and business are marriage partners,' Mr Davis explains. 'They are the original match made in heaven – anywhere, I fear. Conquest breeds cash. But more seriously, there are backward things beginning to happen in Europe, and also in London. The more powerful the old men become, the smaller their souls become, it seems. The hatred for Hebrews is rising up again ...' He shakes his head as if to clear it of this distasteful thought. 'Enough of this unpleasant talk.' He turns outwards, to the whole table, gracious and indisputable gentleman that he is. 'Tonight we make a toast to the

Nor'-West. We toast Australia, and all she has given us. We toast the beautiful women with whom we shall share this meal.'

He looks to Marg as he says this last and my heart dances. Abraham Davis is clinking his glass against Marg Carson's, and she is suddenly so very pretty. She is transformed, and I am so very delighted as I raise my own glass to them, empty but full of love. Yes, love. I remind myself: it is only love that I am feeling, isn't it?

Another wave hits the side of the ship, a bigger one, and our toast is lost in the clinking of cutlery against dinner plates as they slide across the tablecloth; as my shoulder slides into Fin's. The electric lights above us flicker, sizzle.

Someone shouts out across the room: 'Good God, what was that?'

FIN

He knew the sea could sometimes behave erratically in the tropics, heralding a storm well in advance of its sweeping in, as if some deep ocean force spoke to the air in conspiracy, in preparation. No building of cloud, no wind, and yet the sea would churn and the sky would answer with the smell of rain long before a drop had fallen. He smelt it now, as the sea returned to calm once more. He reached for Irene's hand under the tablecloth and he loved that he could feel, in her grasp, that she was unafraid of storms. He loved her more and more.

'To beautiful Australia.' She continued to toast with Abraham Davis. 'Every bump and bristle of the wretched place.'

Her sarcasm was light-hearted, playful, but she meant it. She'd already told him of her hopes of leaving the country herself; to jump out of the fishbowl and swim free – somewhere else, as yet to be determined, most likely beginning with London, then a grand European tour, learn about real life, live – if she could convince her father of the necessity. More fantasy; more and more. And he could only continue his – especially at this present moment, as that policeman, Corporal Buttle, was sitting up the other end of their table. Everywhere Fin turned it seemed he'd run into that damned man – round every corner, behind every door, even sitting behind a pillar in the smoking room on the one occasion he took a stroll through there – he wondered if he really might be following him, watching him, even though the fellow was never interested in giving him more than a polite 'good day'. Buttle sent that mad stare of his up the table at him now, and smiled, stiffly.

Fin pushed away the worry again; policemen must travel on steamships to get to where they're going, too, mustn't they? But as the entrées arrived, he asked Abraham Davis, so that Buttle would hear, too, so that Buttle would be convinced that he was just another businessman travelling on a steamship: 'If you don't mind my enquiring, Mr Davis, how extensive is your fleet of luggers? You know I'm new to the business – perfectly green. The navy has taught me nothing much of any business, and I'm concerned that my investment might be too small and unprofitable.'

Davis smiled at him, the smile of a generous man, giving sage advice to a younger one. 'The first thing I must say to you, Mr Sinclair, is: don't get into this business of pearling. It will consume your whole life, and you will never see your family for more than a few weeks at a time in any year – no better than the navy. But since you want to know, I'll tell you: in the business with my partner, we have thirty luggers and five larger deep-water schooners, and for myself, I have four boats of my own, and I am arranging to purchase more. Of course this means altogether we can bring up a lot of shell, which means that we can easily pay for our costs. For the smaller operators, it can be hard, even with as many as ten boats – I will not paint a pretty picture about it. The cost of labour is very high, especially since the laws against Asians and South Sea Islanders have become more rigorously enforced. That is, if you want to do things correctly – and you should. I get all our labour through an agent in Singapore – a *good* agent, who will not make the men sign impossible contracts where they end up with nothing to show for their work. It's a hard business, I must warn you. Every year one or two men in your employment will die or be badly harmed. They must be fairly paid, and free to leave if or when they must.'

Fin nodded; the more he got to know this pearl dealer, the more he liked him, and the more he regretted his own transience here; his endless trails of deceit. How he wished this particular fantasy was real; he'd spent hours each night after leaving her praying for it to be so, even though, like most who too rarely see fortune swing their way, he wasn't one for prayer. The thought of having a life that was more than just survival, of having a house and a family, was a pretty picture painted on a kite. A kite he had to let go of, along with any dream that Irene could get him out of the stinking morass of shit he was in, but he could not let it go yet. Not for a few days yet.

He asked Abraham Davis now, more to keep the conversation with him going than for any other reason: 'The labour laws are very stringent these days, are they?'

'Oh yes,' said Davis, and he was grave about it. 'The law will turn a blind eye to bad agents so that you can get some divers for practically free, but you can't employ a coloured man onshore – they must stay at sea, and return home, to Malaya, or Japan, or wherever they have come from, when you are finished with them. The White Australia law says they can't live or work in Australia. But of course, it's almost impossible to get a white man to do the work – they would rather starve than dive for shell no matter how well I pay them. And round and round it goes. As I said, it is making it very difficult for smaller operators.'

Davis shrugged then, and continued, graver still: 'For me, I worry more about where these laws are leading. As I said before, things are becoming difficult again for Jews in Europe – will they become difficult soon for me here, too? Any law that says one man is better than another man is dangerous – and stupid. I have a friend in Broome, a Japanese. He is as wealthy as I am, his family is established here, he thinks of himself as an Australian man of the Nor'-West, but these days he can't walk down the street without one of his sons accompanying him, or a business acquaintance, for fear of being arrested as an illegal alien. He is going home to Japan soon – a home he hasn't seen for thirty years. It is madness, these laws. Why turn away successful businessmen and hard workers from your door? Most of all, it makes no business sense. I have written to the government on many, many occasions about all this – I get nowhere. I don't even get a reply. Don't ask me again about the laws.'

The man winced and chuckled at himself then, at some impatience with himself perhaps, and told the ladies at the table: 'Listen to me taking up all the air with talk of business when we should be enjoying our meal. I apologise. Is it any wonder I'm divorced?'

'Mr Davis!' Irene reached across the table and tapped him lightly on the back of his hand as she might a beloved uncle. 'Don't you dare say any such thing ever again. You're a wonderful man. Listen, I'm thinking and wondering and scheming up something here. You do realise you've never invited us to a party at De Vahl,' she turned to Fin, 'that's Mr Davis's famous abode on Roebuck Bay. The parties are famous, too.'

Davis looked at her over his spectacles, happy to be that beloved uncle. 'Well, yes, my dear, that is most likely because you are never in Broome for longer than five minutes.'

'Precisely,' Irene replied, and she was glowing with the fun she was having here. 'I think Marg and I should come to Broome – next month, or early May. What do you say?' She then leant across the table and said to her friend, grin upon scheming grin: 'You know our Mr Davis's soirees are always the talk – and we've never been. How terribly remiss. How on earth could we have allowed that to happen? Or not happen.'

'Now, now, ladies – not so fast,' Davis interjected, but he was having fun, too, pretending reluctance. 'I haven't had a party at De Vahl for an age.'

'So, it's about time, hm?' Irene smoothed the napkin across her lap, decision made. 'I'll see how and when we might come down from Derby and we'll fix it, right?'

'Do I have a choice?' Davis blinked at her.

'Not really.' She blinked back.

Davis turned to Miss Carson then and said: 'Perhaps this is a jolly fine idea. Apart from parties, I hold synagogue at my home on Saturdays. It might be a good opportunity for you to glimpse the divinity at work beneath all my eccentricities, or perhaps simply learn a little about Judaism, if you are really interested ...'

'Oh yes. I am interested in that.' Miss Carson blushed, but as quickly recovered her wit. 'You could show me the mangroves, too, while we're there. Judaism and mangroves – what a holiday hoot that'll be.'

And suddenly they were all laughing uproariously again at their end of the table. A magnificent sound. Fin closed his eyes inside it, just for a moment, free inside this sound.

*

After dinner, Frank Buttle met with Hedley Harris, as he had each night, pausing briefly by the portside rail, just to the rear of the promenade staterooms, only a few yards from where Miss Everley slept, to ask him: 'Still no word?'

Hedley Harris shook his head. 'Not yet.'

The mail picked up from the port of Cossack that afternoon contained no message from the Commissioner's office on the fugitive, McFarland; and none had been received direct by the wireless room on the ship, either. There was only one docking left before Broome now – Port Hedland – and Buttle had begun to wonder what he might do if there was still no word once they did get up to Broome. Find some charge to arrest him on – what? That Buttle himself *might* have overheard this fellow called Sinclair confess to Miss Irene Everley that he was the real estate fraudster McFarland? He could just hear the police prosecutor at Broome asking him, *And how did you come to overhear this?* 'Well, I heard it through the open louvres of her window as she entertained him, alone, in her cabin,' would have to be his reply. And that would be awkward. He didn't want to be the one to expose the extent of Miss Everley's foolishness – ruin her reputation. That wouldn't get him a transfer or promotion anywhere, except for maybe a long and lonely spell up at Cape Leverque.

'You'll find a way to reel him in,' Hedley Harris assured him, before he walked on along the promenade.

And Buttle replied to the near-moonless black of this night: 'I hope so.'

He wasn't all that confident now. He was also beginning to wonder if he might have somehow got this wrong. This McFarland, Sinclair, whoever he was, didn't seem your typical fleecer. There was nothing obviously reprobate about him – he wasn't greasy, and he wasn't too flash. He was a little aloof maybe, a few smooth tickets on himself – pretty much exactly as you would expect an ex-naval officer to be. Davis, the pearler, seemed to think the bloke was fair dinkum, and Davis was nothing but shrewd in all his dealings – not a man to put something over. Perhaps he'd misheard the story through the window that day, with the gulls squawking and his mind demanding to hear what it wanted to hear; perhaps they'd only been talking *about* someone called McFarland.

Maybe Minnie, his wife, was right: he was working too hard. Seeing things that weren't there. But then, he was sure – absolutely certain – that he'd heard the bloke tell Miss Everley he'd been mixed up in that Sydney land scam himself.

Frank Buttle scratched his head. When they pulled into Port Hedland tomorrow, he'd send another telegram to the Commissioner's office. Saying what? He wasn't yet sure.

*

This night, when he came to her cabin, she sat at her little portable typewriter, naked.

'I won't be too long,' she told him. 'I just want to finish this and post the dreadful thing when we get into Heddy tomorrow – get rid of it. This is my last.' She thumped at the keys, talking to herself. 'Promise, promise, promise. Tomorrow, I begin my real life as a real writer of real things.'

'What things?' he asked her, sitting on the edge of the bed, taking off his shoes. 'What will you write about?'

'I don't know.' She shrugged, and then she glanced over her bare shoulder at him. 'You, I suppose. How much I adore you, I suppose, I suppose.'

'That might be dull,' he said, lying back on the bed to watch the fan.

'No,' she told him. 'Not dull. Intensely dirty but far from dull.'

She went back to her typing. Looking at her notebook every so often, staring at the wall for a minute, and then back to thumping the keys again. More and more, he loved her. He loved this – her sitting there working, naked, wanting to be a writer, him calling off the urge to rod her right this minute so she could get on with it.

'Shh, don't laugh,' she said. 'Be a good boy and I'll be good to you in a minute or two.'

It was more like two hours before she was finished, and when she did, she woke him from a doze, telling him: 'Come home to Derby with me, Fin. Don't get off at Broome. Please. Come home and meet my father – Old Hal. You'll love him – everyone does. If he meets you, he'll see. He'll see who you truly are. He'll see this is right. He'll see we make sense.'

'What are you saying?' He wasn't sure if he was still dozing. This was a step too far into reality. This was so impossible, it was absurd: no father would want to meet him, and all he truly was, all he truly carried. This made no sense at all.

'I'm saying, I want you to be with me always.' She sat across his hips; she owned him. 'I'm saying, we go home to Derby, sort things out, and the next time we're back in Broome, hopefully by May, we'll be leaving the country *together*. Unbound and together. We'll travel the world.' She kissed him, this warm and gentle tigress; she kissed him there at the top of his cheek. 'You make me brave, Fin. You make me want to take this leap I need to take – now. Not sometime soon – now. Please, just say yes.'

She swallowed him, and he let her. He said: 'Yes.'

MIYA

My power grew as my yearning grew, so that I could see all who coveted me. I could see the woman start to change his mind. I saw Marg Carson begin to turn Abraham Davis from me. He began to think that perhaps he should take another wife to solve his own strange yearnings; not a stolen pearl.

I saw him with her, there on the ship, walking together in the mornings, and in the evenings, stopping for long moments to gaze at the sea, their heads close together by the rail as he explained to her that pearls were tricks in themselves. 'The lustre, the iridescence, is not a true surface but only the way the light reflects through the nacre – through the layers of shell,' he told her. 'Without the light, a pearl is only a ball of calcium carbonate. Only a piece of oyster grit.'

And she told him, feeling the warmth of his shoulder against hers: 'That's magic enough for me.' Her dislike of pearls was forgotten; her own father's ruin by them, her certainty that they carried only doom – gone.

Perhaps I could have tried to find a way to let them be, these two good people. Perhaps, but this was not a decision for me. It was their concern alone; and they made their choices, both of them. And love, it must be remembered, like any other state of light is subject to the rules: the heat of any meeting of molecules might create a new form, a new force – water, fire, steam – or it might not. Ships might pass in the night, so goes the expression;

opportunities just missed, however beautiful things might have been had they occurred differently. All I can ever do to affect anything is sing, and I could only continue to sing to him, my Mr Davis. I could only continue to draw him by my will, as I was destined to; and as I drew them all.

Now, which one was I up to in my own story? Where had I recounted to? The sixth among my thirteen thieves? That's right – Liebglid, the other Jew. Back then, when I was purchased by him, I was still so new I could barely see beyond a room unless through the touch of another's soul. I hadn't learned yet how to seek them out; hunt for them. But I was learning, all the time, as I grew.

As Liebglid walked towards the beach with me, I sensed those who waited for him. A group of three: one near, on a small boat; two a little further away, on a larger one; and he had already arranged to meet them here, late at night, on some kind of business.

'Get in, then,' a voice beckoned him through the dark; a colourless voice, as detached as it was conniving. 'I'll take you out in the dinghy.' A lamp swung; I saw the pale white face of a man, thin, fair hair streaked across a damp forehead, and I sensed he wasn't aware of my existence. Liebglid wasn't here because of me, I realised; I wasn't being sold.

'No,' Liebglid responded to the man. 'I will look at the pearl here, in the shed.'

'Relax, Yid – reckon we're up to no good, do you?' The pale man goaded him, snorting to signal that it was a joke, but there was no humour in it for either of them. 'Come out onto *The Mist*,' he insisted, and his hand grasped the gunwales of the little row boat they stood near. 'Come and have a drink with us.'

'I've had a drink already, thanks,' Liebglid told him.

And the man insisted once more: 'Have another one. No drink, no pearl. Take it or leave it.'

'All right,' Liebglid acquiesced – he very much wanted to inspect this particular pearl, said to be at least fifty grains and pure white – and so he got into the little boat. As they pushed off the beach and into the shallows, I wailed for him to drop me, to throw me into the sea – I would have upended the boat if I could have at that time, if I'd had any inkling that I might have if I'd tried –

but all I achieved by my wailing was his confusion. 'What did you say?' He stuck a finger in his ear, trying to make sense of the voice he had just heard; my voice.

'I didn't say a word,' the pale man replied and he called out to his partners as they reached the rope ladder of the larger boat at anchor in the bay, the schooner called *The Mist*: 'Hello, my sweethearts, look who we have here.'

The men in the cabin of the schooner were playing a game of some sort, with counters and dice, and they made a show of not caring who it was that had just entered. They talked among themselves, one finishing his turn in the game; they spoke in the language called Tagalog. I didn't know who they were at that first moment, where they were from, but I would learn: they were Manilamen, from the Philippines.

They had brought Liebglid here to sell him a fake – such a fake it was really the glass bead-stopper from a lemonade bottle, the holes either side of it filled with gimcrack paste.

'Show it to me,' Liebglid demanded, feeling the hairs on his arms stand rigid. He knew already that he should not have come here.

'Five hundred,' one of the Manilamen said; the one called Marquez – Pablo Marquez. He was holding the fake before him, but would not let Liebglid touch it.

'I haven't got five hundred on me, only four – four-fifty,' Liebglid said, and it was true; he would have had more had he not bought me earlier.

'Four-fifty?' the other Manilaman said, the one called Simeon Espada, and it was just about the last thing Liebglid heard.

The third man, the pale-faced Englishman who had brought him here and had been standing behind him all the while in the cabin, now raised a hatchet and brought it down on the back of Liebglid's head, smashing his skull. His name was Hagen – Chas Hagen – and his actions in attacking Mark Liebglid were as detached and crude as everything else about him: cold-blooded; casually brutal.

'Search him,' Hagen commanded the Manilamen. 'Take everything he has on him.'

And as they went through his pockets, I began to scream as hard as I could: *Throw him over! Throw him over and into the sea!*

Just as Liebglid, who wasn't yet dead, began bellowing, too: 'Murder! Murder! Help me!'

'Throw him over! Throw him over!' the one called Pablo Marquez heard me and urged the others. 'You killed him! Hagen, you crazy man, why did you kill him? Throw him over!'

And that is what they did. Behind the mangroves, north-east of Roebuck Bay, they threw Mark Liebglid into the sea where he drowned to finish his dying. But not before they had stolen me for themselves.

'Jesus fucking Christmas crackers would you look at that …' The Englishman seemed instantly to forget that he'd just killed a man on finding me in the palm of Simeon Espada's hand.

'*Mutya*,' the Manilamen called me in their wonder, a word that meant 'pearl' and 'sweetheart' and 'enchanted' all in one, in their language. 'We will get more than five hundred for her,' Espada said, as Hagen snatched me away.

But in fact they would get nothing for their Mutya.

As dawn broke and the body of Liebglid washed up with the tide, his head so obviously bashed and broken, witnesses appeared on the beach, and at the police station – so many had heard the screaming in the night: *Murder! Murder!* So many were shocked at the attack on Liebglid, a popular man, a well-liked man. As they gathered, the speculations began, whispers of a cursed, rose-coloured pearl, first from van Gossen and a handful of other dealers throughout the town who thought they might have seen me themselves, whispers that soon swelled to a chorus, and as their thoughts all turned to me, I wailed to all of them, more than a hundred men, that the murder was committed by those aboard *The Mist*: Chas Hagen, Simeon Espada and Pablo Marquez.

Jump into the sea! Jump! I urged Hagen now, all the while as the police moved closer to the schooner in the bay; I screamed to shake and break his own skull. But he only screamed louder himself, ordering his crew to outrun the police launch that neared – a small boat without any motor, only oars and elbow grease. Hopeless in pursuit of a schooner under full sail and with her oil engine sputtering to life. I heard the two constables aboard the launch ruing their situation, ruing that the police were ever ill-equipped, as

I continue to urge Hagen yet harder and louder, *Jump! Jump!* And as I did I found, at last, that I possessed another power, something other than my voice, a force into which could breathe my will: I caused the wind to stop dead still. By luck alone the engine of *The Mist* stalled then, poorly maintained as it was. The schooner was going nowhere.

Marquez was still working frantically to revive the engine, when the police caught up with them, swapping their oars for guns. But just before they boarded the vessel to make their arrests, Hagen, in his grasping attempt to save himself, gave me back to Espada, with every intention of blaming the murder on him. Espada, though, had an even cooler head, and he handed me to a boy, the fourth member of the crew – a boy called Miguel Castro, who was also Espada's young cousin. He was only fifteen, but with his round face and big dark eyes, he looked much younger, and the police, as Espada had hoped, left him alone. He called out to the boy in their own language as the constables dragged him off the boat: 'I will come back for the pearl. I will kill you if you sell it. You will die, I promise.' Little that he knew of just how cursed I was. 'Go ashore. Hide it where no-one will find it,' he demanded of the boy. 'I will come back for the pearl.'

He would never come back for me. Espada, Marquez and Hagen were all condemned to hang. Their stories, to the police and to the court, were a babble of lies upon lies, one pointing his finger at the other. The Manilamen accused Hagen of killing Liebglid because he was a Jew, and he was jealous of the man's popularity and success. Hagen said that Espada and Marquez killed Liebglid for the thrill, because they were bloodthirsty Filipino cannibals. Hagen was still arguing this point as the three were removed to Fremantle Gaol for the gallows there; still arguing as the noose was placed around his neck: 'I am a white man, an Englishman, of course the filthy Manilamen say that I am guilty with them. Of course – because the Manilamen are liars.' I saw the dank coldness of the England he had come from; I saw the hungry faces of the family he'd deserted there; I saw that he had left them because he believed he deserved better. I saw the plainness of his motives: greed. Only greed, selfish greed. None of the thieves were sorry for what they had done, except perhaps for Marquez, but life was too cheap for him to give even his own death too much thought. He hoped the devil would not deal with him too cruelly; he made the sign of the cross, of his Catholic faith, as the trapdoor opened, and it was done.

I felt no sorrow for them either; I had my own sorrows to count. Young Miguel Castro had done as he was bid, immediately taking me ashore to find a hiding place for me. Scared and lonely without his older cousin, and too terrified of being caught to hear my pleas that he should best hide me in the sea, with trembling, hurried hands he wrapped me in a rag and stuffed me between two bricks in the foundations under the back wall of the Star Hotel, into a space where the mortar had crumbled away. He couldn't think what else to do.

He felt my song only as some sound of horror within, and he gave me a Spanish name to match it – 'Ampollo del Diablo' – the devil's blister. Appropriate, it seemed, that day there in Broome, that warm winter's day in the year 1905 on which the legend of my curse was born into the world of men, in all its babble of stories.

I had the next five years to listen to every one of them, stuck there as I was under the wall of that hotel. The stories churned and swirled throughout the Nor'-West and beyond. I was a maharaja's ransom, I was a dragon's eye. I was evil. I was beautiful. I was hotly desired. But no matter how I cried there, no matter the winds I brought, or the surf I taught myself to pound onto the shore, no-one heeded my entreaties. No matter how I called up through the boards of that hotel to tell them exactly where I was, no-one believed I was there. Why would they? It was not a very thrilling story. To any passing soul I begged to listen to me, it did not seem possible, either, that I was there, right there, under his feet all that time.

I could only wait then, and wait, as my power grew, and grew, with each turning of the moon, as I called and called to Miguel Castro to come back for me.

IRENE

I wake and find him sleeping beside me, and I am washed through with the rush of a thousand miracles. That he is here, and I am, too. That I want this to be forever, every night and every day. I do. I do. I don't understand why, but I do.

I want the years ahead, each moment, together; I want to watch beauty fade from his face, replaced and replaced by deeper beauties. I want to find truth after truth in him, every detail. I want to hold the small boy that is him in my arms and make him laugh and dance and play as he was never allowed then; as he is allowed here, with me. I can barely believe these thoughts, but that's only because I've never really had them until now. I've never loved before, not like this. I am twenty-seven years old, and I am in love. I am in love with someone who might even love me back. Dad's got to be happy with that. Progress.

It's even a little cooler today. The breeze through the louvres is heavenly on my skin. Heaven on earth. I am in Arcady, and my prince sleeps beside me, on this dawn of the seventh day together. And thus heaven and earth were finished, said the Lord, and many other things I can't quite remember from all those compulsory lessons in conventional mythological allegory we were forced to sit through once upon a time at school. I do recall, however, that God sent a mist across the world to create all the trees and the flowers. It must have been this lovely, cooling mist. Or we really have travelled beyond Olympus; beyond the Garden of Eden, too. We are somewhere no-one but us has ever been.

Or will be when all temporal affairs are tidied up and we are free to leave for whatever our tomorrows hold. I'm yet to write my farewell note to Phil Oswald at *Aus Life*, and I must do it now. Not to be delayed any longer. Because I am posting my final column to him today. This afternoon in Heddy. *Oh, dearest Phil, it's been such fun but it's time …* Time to get up and write the thing now, and don't think about how put out he will be when he receives it – not at the idea of losing me, but at having to find another writer, and undoubtedly a male one, whom he'll have to pay three times more in peanuts than he did me. Ah well, all good things must come to an end.

Except for me and Fin.

I stand up and reach for my kimono wrap in this glorious cool air, and as I do, I see myself in the mirror above the washbasin, and my hair is wild with electricity. A halo? I don't know about that. But I am definitely mad. I make a mad lady face at myself inside my electric hair: yes, I am delirious. And I am ready to leap, cloud to cloud, today.

FIN

'Look,' she said to him, through the mirror, when she saw that he had opened his eyes. 'I know who I am with this mad hair today. I am Aphrodite. I am Botticelli's Venus rising from the sea. See?'

And this was exactly why he couldn't go on with the dream. He knew the names of these characters she spoke of, from having read them, heard them, here and there – Aphrodite, Botticelli, Venus, Endymion, Keats – but he didn't know them as she did. They were all near meaningless to him, symbolic only of a level of education he would never receive. He hadn't studied at university or spent time in Melbourne art galleries; he wasn't schooled beyond Third Form, for all that he had got near top marks in Geography and Mathematics when he was there. He was never going anywhere but the Braefield Industrial whatever marks he'd got. He was not going anywhere with Irene Everley now. He was going to get out of her life as quickly and as kindly as he could. Her father might have been the self-made, salt-of-the-earth sort of man his daughter said he was, but he was also one of the most powerful cattlemen in Western Australia – Fin had read all about that in *The Past and the Future*, too. Men such as Harold Wellington Everley had made themselves and the Kimberley what they are today: rich. And with their bare hands. Such men, or any kind of men, do not give their daughters to runaways who have criminal charges hanging over their heads. Not even in the most fantastic of stories.

He was going to pack and leave the ship today, and never see her again. She did not deserve the trouble he would bring her if he stayed.

'You're extraordinary,' he told her, and he kissed her, and then as he began to dress he said: 'I'll see you at dinner, then?'

'Oh?' she said, taming her hair, pinning it up. 'That's a long time away. What am I going to do without you for the next eight hours?'

'Eight hours, that's a blink,' he said, feeling the wrench of it already, telling his shoelaces: 'I've got some correspondence I must attend to. Might take a while.'

'That's funny.' She smiled. 'Me, too, then I'm off into Heddy – post office and some shopping I want to do. So, dinner it is. I suppose you'll need this little while at the pen breaking it off with all your other lovers, hm?'

'That's right,' he said, and he didn't look at her again, for his eyes had filled with tears. 'See you.' He closed her door behind him.

He was not Endymion, the mortal so handsome the moon fell in love with him, or so she told him. He was Icarus; he knew that one: you couldn't read an article on whatever new feat of aviation had lately ended in disaster without some reference to that unfortunate fool. With his wings made of wax, with his hopes too high, he had flown too close to the sun. It was over.

*

'You have word?' Frank Buttle turned as soon as he heard Hedley Harris say his name, seeking him out in the smoking room, as he looked out the window over the long jetty and into Port Hedland.

'Yes – here. At last.' The purser held out the message slip.

And Buttle read it: *Keep suspect in sight at all times. Sgt E. Jackson will meet off ship in Broome to identify as Finlay McFarland and arrest.*

That immediately rankled: Buttle wanted this arrest for himself – he needed it. But as usual, the boys in Broome would take the credit. He sighed. He might still look into that transfer to the South Australian force, of course, but with little or no endorsement from his superiors here in Western Australia and nothing to distinguish his service record but his bush skills and horsemanship, he'd possibly remain a corporal, shooting dingoes at the boundary fences of Andamooka. A long way from Adelaide.

Unless he could think of some charge to arrest McFarland on now.

Indecent assault. The lie swirled round his mind, and not for the first time, although it took on some urgency here. He could arrest this McFarland-Sinclair bloke under suspicion of molestation: that would protect Miss Everley's reputation, as an unwilling party, and, given the seriousness of the fraud charges, it was one he thought he might just make stick. Once it was all exposed, once the blinding scales were removed from her eyes, Miss Everley would probably be only too happy to cry foul, so he thought. There was his promotion and his new and more salubrious posting; there was his family's future security. If he could dare to take that gamble. If he could risk humiliating Miss Everley. If he could go through with the lie. Lying, even for the greater good, did not sit well with Frank Buttle, which was another reason he'd been overlooked so long for advancement. And something else to think about. Perhaps it was time to start playing the game as everyone else did. He might never become a Catholic, but maybe he could learn to get around the rules like one.

'Is there anything you'd like me to do?' Harris asked beside him.

'No,' said Buttle. 'Just continue to keep note of where and when you see him about. Have you seen him this morning?' Buttle hadn't seen him since breakfast, when the man had briefly appeared in the dining room to grab himself a bread roll and an apple; he'd looked to be at a dash somehow, perhaps on his way out into port for the day, which was why Buttle had stationed himself here, where he could see the ship's comings and goings.

Hedley Harris looked out at the jetty, out at the small town beyond it that sat on the edge of the wide, lonely desert, and he said to the policeman: 'No. No, I haven't seen him yet today.'

*

Finlay McFarland looked back at the ship from the room he'd just booked into, at the Pier Hotel, and then he resumed pacing the floor.

How could he do this to her?

Perhaps she was right: she could work it all out, with her connections and her money. She could do what she liked. What was he doing running away from the chance she was offering him, the rope she was throwing him? So what if he had to spend a year or two in prison? So what? It couldn't be worse than any other institution he'd known. He'd take a few beatings for her; he could take whatever might come if need be.

But his thoughts only ran round again to her, the harm all this would cause her, and he couldn't put her through it. The likely way things would go for them would be that she'd take him home to meet her father and her father would personally throw him to the sharks, piece by piece – and then a newspaper would get wind of any gossip and drag her down with him. That's the way things always go, don't they? That's what happens to women who step out of line. And besides all that, he'd only known her a week – this was past ridiculous. His whole life was past ridiculous.

He was the one that had to go, and take his misfortune with him. If he stayed, at best she'd only tire of him within another week or two anyway, once the excitement of her easy conquest wore off, once she got bored with her bit of rough. Wouldn't she?

He had until about ten am the next morning to be sure of his decision. The *Koombana* would miss the tide this afternoon, he knew; it would be a big new-moon tide, too, no avoiding it, and so the ship would dock here until then.

Wherever here was. Port Hedland: a haphazard collection of tin shacks strung out behind two towering pubs, servicing a long jetty that curved out into its shallow, narrow-necked bay. All dock and no town, surrounded by dull, tawny sand the colour of a rusty post, which somehow looked as thirsty as the low scrub that was strewn about in frowsy, indiscriminate clumps. No real attempt at marking out anything like a road here, either, because camel trains don't need them, he supposed. No unsuspecting visitor would guess at the money that came through this place, on and off this jetty and in and out of the cargo sheds that lay beyond the customs house, which was also a shed, as it seemed was the new railway station. Enormous wealth and flimsy impermanence at every port along the west coast.

Australia. Such a strange land. He would miss her and her careless, carefree contradictions. He'd been so sure, only a few months ago, that he had found a home here, that he would buy that little plot at Narrabeen, north of Sydney, and live barefoot on the white sand there every Sunday. Marry a girl. Build up some money in the bank. A couple of fat, laughing babies making sandcastles on the beach. Just a dream. It always had been. Not his to hold.

Take me into the sea …

He thought he heard the voice again on the blustering breeze that made the curtains billow in his room.

Return me to the sea …

It sounded like the wheeling, keening cry of a bird, high up.

Throw me into the sea …

The breeze was really picking up, gusting up under the tin awning of the verandah outside, and so he closed the window, and yet he wondered if that voice was more than his imagination crying kite-like in the air, but some advice come forth from deep within: telling him he should throw himself into the sea and be done with it. For then, and only then, his running would surely stop.

How would it feel, he wondered now with sharper clarity, how would it truly feel, to walk out to the end of the long jetty before him, and slip into that warm and sparkling sea? If nothing else, he would be free. Wouldn't he?

MIYA

It was not until young Miguel Castro was preparing to be married that he returned to Australia from the Philippines. 'I will make some good money for us,' he told his girl, Rita. 'I will only be gone three months, not even the whole pearling season.' He loved her with everything he had, and he had lived a blameless, honest and loving life since returning to Manila five years earlier. He went to mass every week, sometimes twice; he honoured every wish and expectation of his parents. He had purchased a small fishing boat with another cousin and they did well from it. They didn't make a fortune, but they did well enough.

Still, Miguel wanted more, for his Rita, and for himself. He wanted wealth, he wanted the status that wealth would bring. He wanted a bigger boat; perhaps ten boats. He wanted the best house for his wife. And he was prepared to seek out the devil to get it. To return for me – the Ampollo del Diablo he'd left under the wall of the Star Hotel in Broome all those years ago. He was half expecting that I would not be there, long found and sold on. He was half expecting to return to Manila with only a decent roll of cash from diving for the well-paying pearl masters of Piggot & Co.

But he found me, sure enough, on the bright-lit night of the full moon in June 1910, he snuck onshore from his lugger, and found me there in the wall at the rear of the Star Hotel, wrapped in that same rag he had concealed me in. His hand trembled this time with excitement as he held me. At first, he didn't know what to do;

and he couldn't understand the violent crashing that came into his head as anything but the devil himself roaring at him. It was me, of course; caught in my own excitement, I was shouting incoherently. What was I hoping he would do? Take fright and run screaming into the water with me? Possibly. He had wits enough about him, though, to go straight into the front bar of the hotel, where the dealers did all manner of business every evening of the season.

Miguel knew little of current prices or who best to approach, he'd been out of the business too long and even when he had worked here before he'd been a boy, so he hoped only to sell to the first buyer he found, and get out of there as quickly as possible. The hotel looked familiar when he entered, even some of the people seemed to look the same as they had five years ago. Nothing much had changed in Broome, except that it was now much more strictly illegal for him to be onshore; a policeman would soon come to shove him back onto his lugger.

'What do you want in here, feller?' A large white man with a great fat belly moved towards him as soon as he was in the door, and Miguel jumped with fright.

'I – I ...' he stammered. His fear caused him to forget the few words of English he had, but he thought of his Rita at home in Manila, how proud she would be when he returned with their money, and he found the only important ones he needed at this moment: 'I have pearl. You dealer?'

'You have pearl, do you, little feller?' The fat man laughed, not unkindly, but he narrowed his eyes hungrily. 'Well, don't stand there waiting for the coppers to come and have a look, too. Show me what you got.'

Miguel opened his hand, and the fat man almost shouted when he saw me, pulling his shock into a whisper just in time: 'Well, fuck me.'

The fat man dragged Miguel outside then by the back of his neck, and Miguel thought he was done for. He would have pleaded with the man for his life, told him that he could have me for nothing, he would have thrown me at him if he hadn't been so completely paralysed with fear.

'I'll give you a thousand for it.' The man hissed through the dark, there around the darkest side of the hotel.

Miguel was shaking so much now that the man presumed he was shaking his head in refusal.

'Fifteen hundred and no more,' the man offered again.

And this time Miguel managed to nod: 'Good. *Opo. Sí.* Yes.' He agreed in every language he knew.

The fat man was called Kerrigan, I found as I searched him, scrabbling through my own sense of the dark for his soul. He reached into his trouser pocket and pulled out the biggest roll of cash that Miguel had ever seen, and he counted out the deal in fifty-pound notes. Miguel did not care to count them himself.

When Kerrigan said: 'Now fuck off and don't come back here – ever,' Miguel had no trouble obeying the command. He ran for his dinghy on the beach; he would have rowed himself back to the Philippines if he hadn't run into his lugger first.

Back on board, he fell to his knees in gratitude. He thought he had got away with it; he thought of how happy Rita would be: he would build her that beautiful home; he would buy ten boats; he would buy his father a new boat as well. I thought perhaps young Miguel had got away with it, too, but he hadn't. When he eventually returned to Manila a few months later, his parents threw a party that first night he was home, and as the celebrations continued long into the night, one of his aunts mistakenly left a pot of cooking oil on the hot wood stove and it caught fire. All in the house were killed; Miguel and his Rita, too. I heard their screams across all the oceans between us, such was the reach of my power now.

The man called Kerrigan seemed impervious to it, though. He might have shared Miguel Castro's Catholic religion, but he had none of his soul. The essence of him appeared to me as a remnant of string snagged upon the face of a vast brick barricade. Stanley Kerrigan had been a policeman of high rank, an inspector, but was lately retired. He'd made his living, one way or another, through illegal dealings all his life; I could never quite see what had caused his early retirement, but there was violence involved, glimpses of angry men carrying spears; barking dogs; gunshots; the exchange of cash tied up in a cotton sugar bag. I could never quite see him at all.

Kerrigan had no interest in my unusual beauty, or my story. As soon as I was in his possession, he shut me into that black box, that small, ordinary display box of silk over card, and then he locked me in his safe, at his home on Cable Beach Hill over Broome. From there, I shouted and shrieked so much that the housekeeper and several guests who would often come and go from his home were regularly unnerved. I shattered glasses; I slammed doors in the dead of dead-still nights. But Kerrigan never flinched; he never heard a word.

He waited just over a year for the right buyer, before singling out Jarrod Neath, the manager of the Union Bank at Port Hedland. He made a special journey south to meet with him, disguising his purpose by travelling overland in his motorcar, visiting associates along the way, telling them all he was going to Port Hedland to attend the opening of the rail line to Marble Bar. It was worth all this trouble to him – and to me. Neath was the perfect mark: middling in his career, he was bored, stuck in this coarse and loutish outpost, and he was both vain and insecure with it. When Kerrigan took him into his confidence, over the whisky they shared under the verandah of the Pier Hotel, telling him that he had the legendary cursed and rose-coloured pearl up for offer, Neath was flattered, and at the same time envious. As soon as I whispered to him, *I can be yours*, Jarrod Neath wanted me. He would have me, and whatever advantage he thought I might bring him.

He paid £5000 for me: £937 of his own money, and the rest embezzled from the bank. He took the black box from Kerrigan and put me in the drawer of his desk, there in his office at the bank, and there I would wait almost another year until he found someone to single out himself. Someone vulnerable. I searched for him, too. And we found him together: Abraham Davis.

Jarrod Neath had known the pearling magnate for quite some time, as Abraham Davis often stopped in to make a withdrawal at the bank whenever he found himself in Port Hedland with pearls on the table and too few funds in his pocket. He knew all about the drawn-out divorce, too – how humiliating that must have been – and Neath would be the one to send him a timely diversion, a little excitement. He wasn't sure, of course, if one as scrupulous as Abraham Davis could be so lured, but he thought he might as well give it a try – he needed someone with deep pockets for the price he'd be asking.

In the meantime, as I waited, there in the drawer, I stretched my will as I had never yet done. Before returning to Broome, Stanley Kerrigan went yachting with an old acquaintance around Turtle Island, just to the north-east of Port Hedland, and while he was out there, I called the swell up from the cool, dark heart of the Indian Ocean to smash a wave against that yacht. I swept him from the deck and I dragged him down to the clam beds below.

Jarrod Neath had barely required any subtlety in his actions, either. He sent a letter to Abraham Davis, to his off-season home in Melbourne, a prattling letter, only fishing for a response, saying he'd heard a rumour that a pearl by the name of 'Rosy' had come onto the snide market, and that it was said to be that cursed pink pearl of Nor'-West infamy. Would he ever be tempted by something like that? And Mr Davis replied straight back, with a one-word telegram, saying only: *PERHAPS*. Of course he did: because as soon as I felt the first twinges of his interest, I began to call him across the miles – to convince him that he wanted me more than anything.

Oh how I regretted what I sought to do.

But I had to. I had to call Mr Davis onto the ship. Onto the *Koombana*. I had to call this final thief to me, this kind and thoughtful man in the expensive suit, his moustache unkempt. There was no-one else. The moon was fast waning to its blackest; this new moon would travel closest to the earth for some time – closest to me – to fill me with power, ever greater power. Time was now. If I missed this chance, this moon, this tide, how much more monstrous would my power grow before the next? What would I need to do, before I found another man to listen to me? I had to find myself in this man's pocket, any pocket, on that ship.

TWIST

What immortal hand or eye
Could frame thy fearful symmetry?

IRENE

The sea is a jewel in this late-afternoon light, so green against the deep-blue clouds blooming at the north horizon, I can hardly take my eyes off it. Rippled jade, under the flurries of the wind. I want to take off my shoes and stockings and walk upon it, with my hair flying wild about me.

I look to the west, back towards the ship, to the bright lowering sun, and I wonder if Fin is looking at this sea, too, or if he's still dozing. The note he left for me, the corner of it just sticking out from under his door, said, *Go away – I'm asleep. You've exhausted me. Fx.*

How many hours to go until dinner? I look at my wrist watch: too many. It's only five o'clock. I'm glad no-one can hear my thoughts: I've gone from mad to embarrassing, wandering around like a lost housewife all afternoon. After kissing farewell to *Aus Life* at the post office, I spent an hour in Brodie's store lingering over the frilly smalls, and finding nothing lovely enough to match my mood or grab for my sisters, no books of interest there, either, and then I spent another good hour playing with all the toys out the back and purchasing half a dozen assorted tin wind-ups and string puppets for the Derby horde. I can't wait to see them all now. Can't wait to show them my handsome, curious stranger, too. *Surprise!*

I wonder if he can ride a horse; I wonder if mine, Freckle, will like him.

God help me.

I've just kissed goodbye to the small shred of a career I had. Have I done the right thing? Yes. I have. I must have. By May, when my last 'Purple Daze' appears in print, I will be on my way to the rest of the world – with Fin. And I won't ever have to re-read the dreadful little verse I ended my column with. *The tide swells, the storm uncurls – What is love but grit for pearls?* Too late to change it. Oh dear; oh well. Bon voyage.

Filling in sliver after sliver of time until we might get on with it, I wander over to the handful of Afghan hawkers behind the Esplanade Hotel, to see if there might be something fun over there. 'Good evening, miss,' I'm greeted by the first of them, smiling at me under his turban, robes billowing in the breeze. 'All good quality, all one hundred percent genuine gold, silver, precious stones.'

I laugh, and he laughs back. We both know the story here. But I look at his trays of earrings and bangles anyway, laid out at the back of his van as they are with his selection of one hundred percent magic carpets, and smiling up at me is a pair of outstanding paste-gem danglers – the purple 'stones' so lurid, I'm not sure what they're attempting to be, and the gold so yellow, it might rub off in my fingers as soon as I pick them up. One of the camels brays from where he sits beside the van in the sand: *You must have them.* Perhaps as a final, violently violet souvenir of all my time here? No: they are so hilariously loud and gaudy, I think immediately that my sister Oceanna must have them. She will gasp the loudest – in happy horror.

'How much, please?' I ask the hawker.

'One pound and four shillings,' he says. 'All genuine.'

All genuine robbery. But I love them too much, so I buy them from him. I am envisioning Ocea raiding the dress-up box for something to wear with them – eye-patch and red velvet bustier, chasing the children round the yard with Rupert's wooden cutlass: *Beware the Pirate Mummy! Arrrrrgh!* Too wonderful.

'Thank you, miss. Good evening and safe travels to you,' the hawker bids me a hearty adieu, and that's all my shopping done.

As I turn back for the jetty, the breeze momentarily whisks up a willy-willy, a ballerina wisp of sand coiled almost rooftop high that quickly collapses into stillness once more. I stand there and watch it return to dust, and then I don't know what to do. I suppose I could go and annoy Marg, and possibly Mr Davis, too, wherever they are. Or I could go and have a bath before dinner. Yes, that's what I shall do ...

The twine from my packages of toys is cutting into the fingers of my left hand as I start back for the ship, and the sharp afternoon sun is absolutely blinding no matter how I put my other hand up for shade against it, or kink the brim of my hat. As I look away from the sun, near the corner of the Esplanade I see a black face: a man, shirtless and shoeless, lighting a cigarette, watching me. Me being a pathetic white woman tottering up the dusty road. The way the natives look at you sometimes – I know they want us all dead and gone. I don't blame them. I smile; he looks through me. They do give you a shiver.

I keep walking, a little more quickly, and as I go I hear something clank behind me; the sound of a chain thudding and dragging – perhaps belonging to a bullock dray? I turn to see what it is, but even as I'm doing so, I am instinctively getting out of the way.

I don't get to see what it might be, though. The wind makes a sudden and more concerted effort to distract me, whipping my hat off my head, flinging half my hair from its pinnings, too, and right across my eyes. The heel of my left shoe seems to plunge into nothing as I spin around, off kilter – arms flailing about, searching for something to grab hold of to stop my fall, such as the fence of the cattle pen I thought was here a second ago, where it usually is, behind the jetty. I can hear the cattle bellowing, that way they do at the light on being led off the ship, and I see them as the wind returns my sight – a pretty load of Aberdeen-Angus heifers, awaiting tick inspection – as I continue to fall through the air.

Until I feel the fencepost of the cattle pen go whack into the back of my head.

'Miss! Madam! Are you all right?'

A man in a broad felt hat is standing over me as I lie sprawled, my left foot twisted under me, my head throbbing with a series of small but painful explosions, and the middle finger of my left hand really stinging now from being sliced by the package twine. Behind him, I see another black face staring, not at me but into the sun, as he passes by, shuffles by, clank, thud, chained between two other men. Oh. I look the other way, into the pen, and one of the heifers lowers her broad velvet snout towards me and snorts: *Yes, a most inelegant display.*

I tell her and the man in the hat: 'I'm all right, I think, but I might need some assistance getting up.'

The man, possibly the tick-inspection vet, leans down to me, saying something soothing like, 'Don't worry,' but I don't quite hear him, and I'm not worried. I'm wondering, somewhat deliriously, why we have such a preference for beef when we are surrounded always by so many fish. Fish everywhere: I am falling through a great shoal of them, swishing all around me. I am falling again. Falling far, far away ...

FIN

He pulled the shutters closed across the window as the breeze increased again to gusts that came like a pulse now, the ragged edges of a distant storm flicking at the coast as it spun somewhere out to sea.

The wind continued to call to him through the slats, but as the hours unfolded, its insistence that he throw himself into the sea began to sound more and more like, *Go to Irene.*

The shutters only rattled, and rattled, stoking his agitation, tossing him again to and fro amid his uncertainty – until a terrible realisation struck him. When he'd left the ship this morning, he'd smuggled himself away as any seaman, under his cloth cap, disguised as no-one in particular in the canvas shirt and denim strides he'd worn a week ago in Kalgoorlie. He'd left just about everything else in the cabin, taking only what he could stuff into his rucksack, making this decision as final as he could. But here, with all his second thoughts around him, he saw that when they eventually opened that cabin door, sometime tonight, or maybe tomorrow, and found all of his belongings there, it could well be presumed that he'd done away with himself, as people occasionally do at sea, because the sea is there, for those who are called to it. And he couldn't do this worst of all things to Irene. No, not when her mother —

You've exhausted me, he had written in that note he'd left her. *I'm asleep.* Too close to the words her mother had used in that miserable excuse for goodbye. What had possessed him to write such a thing?

He left the room at once then; he left the hotel and walked out into the night. It was late, about nine, and the night was black, dead black, with the new moon and the heavy sky.

He couldn't wound her this way. He had to leave her with something of his love; for once in his life he would not vanish without a word. He knew he would carry the face of this woman with him always, no matter how hard he might try to resist looking over his shoulder. He would carry her smile, her laughter, and after this night, no doubt, her anger. He would go to her now; he would tell her he was sorry; he would explain.

Perhaps find another way to – could they find another way, to be together? He put his head down into the wind and he strode towards the ship.

*

'Excuse me, Mr Davis?' Hedley Harris reluctantly interrupted the man. Abraham Davis was sitting in amiable conversation with Miss Margaret Carson in the saloon again, after dinner, some pleasant thing going on between them there, but Hedley had to tell him: 'Mr Neath has arrived – for your meeting?'

Hedley was curious as to what sort of a meeting the pearler and the banker would be having so late in the evening, why Mr Neath had seemed so intent on discretion, and he was annoyed with himself that he'd let that curiosity become obvious in his questioning tone – it was none of his business. He made a slight bow by way of apology.

Abraham Davis hadn't even noticed it; he'd sprung to his feet. 'Is that the time? Please excuse me, Miss Carson. As expected, I must away, have this business over and done with. Perhaps, in the morning, we will continue our discussion over coffee – about ten, as we push out?'

'Oh yes, good evening, Mr Davis – see you then.' She smiled in a teasing, jovial way. 'Perhaps.'

Hedley Harris smiled, too: he did enjoy a little shipboard romance such as this – a decorous one. Not like some others. There was something about Mr Davis and Miss Carson that made them a matching pair, a certain sturdiness, good humour – and most remarkably, they each had the same pale, flawless skin, the kind of skin that almost glowed.

'Mr Harris, could you please retrieve my case from the safe and bring it to my cabin?' Mr Davis asked, his words clipped, a low rumble as he passed, a man with important things to attend to.

And Hedley Harris followed him out. 'Of course, sir.'

*

The anxiety had left him, blasted away by the wind this night, eclipsed by Margaret Carson's cheerful, sparkling eyes, by her quick mind and her generous nature. She wasn't Jewish, but was that such a bar when she might be happy to begin the study necessary to become one? She seemed so ready, so enthusiastic for some kind of learning, something to get that mind of hers well absorbed by. It was a shame that her father had not had the means or the inclination to send her to university. But then, if he had, perhaps she would already be married.

Was he seriously considering ...?

It would seem so. He chuckled to himself as he continued to walk towards his cabin. His ex-wife, Cecily, had been such a beauty – and such a fake. Her name wasn't even Cecily – it was Sarah. When he looked back now, he could see she had always been looking for something else – looking for it in her own business, and in a more handsome man. She could have it; he finally made peace with her there as he walked, because he could have something that suited him better, too. Margaret Carson: she would be a wonderful friend and, with God's blessing, a wonderful mother. *Perhaps*. All those months of angst and shame seemed such a waste of time in this new light.

And the idea of making a £20,000 deal on a snide pearl seemed simply bizarre. Some strange reverie. Only Neath really was about to come to his door with this pearl. Abraham had thought it an invention of the collective Nor'-West imagination until he'd received that letter; he was intrigued. Over the years, he'd heard it referred to as the Roseate Pearl and Pink Wonder; he'd heard so many different stories about its curse. But he'd never himself imagined it was real, until – what? What had got hold of him, he couldn't now say.

'Mr Davis.'

He turned at the cabin door, at the sound of his name.

It was Jarrod Neath, walking towards him down the corridor. A tall man with a loping stride and dark, greying hair; always attired, somewhat pretentiously, in pinstripe. The wind had made a mess of his pomade-slicked hair.

Abraham did not want what he was selling. He wasn't in need of escape any longer. He didn't want to strike out against Cecily. He didn't want to dissolve his long partnership with Rubin, either: the man was his sister Rebecca's husband; the man was his friend, and remained so despite the geographical distance between them; it had always been a successful partnership in all ways. He didn't need to reassert control – over anything. He wasn't in search of a thrill. He'd found a better one.

'Good to see you, old fellow.' He stretched out his hand to shake Neath's, nodding at Hedley Harris, who followed with the case.

He would still look at this Rosy – he would never not want to look at a pearl. Perhaps he would buy her for Margaret Carson. Abraham Davis might have been old-fashioned and inclined to over-working, but he was still foolish enough, and honey-hearted enough, to buy a girl a pretty thing. He smiled to himself recalling how adamant she had been that he purchase that specific piece of amethyst for Dorothy at Onslow, her eye so keen for the beauty it held, so keen to see it given to another. Margaret deserved something in return, a sign, an indication of —

No, he told himself as he ushered the banker into the cabin. Don't be so foolish – not yet. This pearl – it was too much to be a token. And it was tainted. Too tainted for her.

*

The three prisoners sat silent in the dimness of the main-deck cattle stalls. Although these stalls amidships were empty now of cattle, they still stank of manure, and over that stink lay the smell of fresh bread coming from the baker's ovens across the other side of the companionway. Uncomfortable in every way, and Frank Buttle was growing impatient.

Late this afternoon, after a pointless day of searching for McFarland through the town, the corporal had just found the note under the bastard's door, saying he was busy sleeping – the note that was signed off with the initial 'F', giving him some proof of identity at last, too – when he'd then been called away to shepherd these three unfortunates aboard: a Malay, a Jap and a young Abo lad, who were bound for Broome and an appearance in court. The Malay and the Jap had tried to kill each other in one of the opium shacks behind the beach north of the town, drawing attention to themselves and their illegal status; both no doubt would be deported within the week, nothing unusual there. The Aborigine was something else altogether. When the Port Hedland constable had handed Frank the paperwork on the prisoners, he'd said: 'Try to get the blackfeller's name off him, will you? He won't speak.'

Who cares? was Frank Buttle's first thought; his second was to request that the ship's chief steward, Johnson, take a break from his supervision of bread-making to come and relieve him here so that he could attend to other matters – that matter being keeping up surveillance of his much bigger fish. To the long-suffering corporal, this was the problem with the whole Nor'-West. They were so short on staff all the time, one man gets sick or called away – as has happened in Hedland this afternoon – and the justice system falls over. The one who should be following the tail of a fair-dinkum criminal at large ends up tending to three others of little consequence. And waiting for about four hours now for assistance. It wasn't the chief steward's responsibility – of course he'd be busy with work of his own – and it wasn't Hedley Harris' either, as he'd be busy, too. But for Christ's sake, somebody just needed to sit here and watch them. The prisoners were chained – shackled at their feet, their hands, and to each other by their necks – and they were sat on a fixed bench in this stall, chained in turn to the bars of it. They weren't going anywhere without a great deal of difficulty.

Frank looked at the Abo lad again. Poor young bloke sitting there in his chains – between the Malay and the Jap, to keep them separated. Not ideal. Frank had had to give the Malay a clip already for carrying on in his gobbledygook way, threatening the Jap. The black lad sat there in his trance through it all. Frank wondered where Aborigines went when they did that, but he didn't wonder very deeply, never enough to ask.

He asked the lad instead, again: 'Come on, mate. Give us your name. It's not going to make it any better or worse for you, just easier for everyone else.'

Especially for whatever official of the Protector of Aborigines would be looking at this case in Broome – if it was a do-gooder, there'd be accusations of police brutality before they got off the ship, never mind got his name. Those soul-saving evangelical types only ever made things worse by meddling further in what couldn't be fixed by meddling of any kind, as far as Frank Buttle was concerned.

'Come on, young feller,' he tried again.

But it was no use. The Aborigine continued to sit there and stare ahead into the gloom of the cattle stall opposite, unresponsive. Frank had another good look at him: the lad was fit, healthy; he had traditional scars on his chest, like claw marks coming down over each of his shoulders. He'd been charged with destruction of property – spearing cattle – and he'd go for a spell in prison for it, not that prison was of any use to an Abo, either. They never learned.

'Righto then, we'll do things your way.' Frank sat back down again on his stool, and wished he'd brought a book to read. He looked across at the lad again and shook his head, baffled.

Why did they keep spearing the cattle and ending up here? He knew they weren't stupid. He'd been dealing with these blacks for almost two decades – since the one they called Jandamarra went rogue and took on the police in the nineties, spearing more than cattle over his three-year guerrilla war across the southern stretches of the Kimberley. Frank Buttle had worked with some other brilliant trackers over the years, too; all of them disappearing off the job after a while, gone walkabout, gone wanda, gone home, wherever home might have been. He knew any man who could survive out there in the desert – never mind for thousands of generations – was far from stupid. What was it that they didn't understand about not spearing cattle, though – and about getting locked up if you do?

Things had been hard inland, Frank knew as well as anyone: the unreliable rainfall for the last four or five years, bringing disappointing wet seasons, was now looking like dug-in drought; from the Pilbara up through the Kimberley, creeks remained dry, waterholes were emptied out, everything was parched when at this time of year the desert should have greened up. When he'd left Derby at Christmas, he'd just come in from the police outpost on the Lennard south of the Napier Range, checking on things out there beyond Everley Station before taking his holidays, and the only clouds in the sky were blood red and black from rampaging fire, bilging up above the walls of the river gorge. Still, the Aborigines there were hardly starving: there was plenty of kangaroo about; he'd watched a mob of more than a hundred come in to drink at the river's edge – in fact, they were making themselves pests, competing for feed with the cattle.

It didn't make sense to Frank Buttle. This lad in front of him had maybe seen a brother or two get shot out there, as well. And what for? If they were really struggling, if they'd gone somewhere like Everley's with their hands out, they'd have probably walked away with a carcass butchered neatly for them, so they'd bugger off quietly. Frank shook his head again: men like Everley were a bit too few and far between. It wasn't Frank Buttle's question to answer, anyway; not his land to fight over. Only a job to do.

'Corporal – Butters, is it?' Johnson, the chief steward, had finally arrived to assist him, and was none too pleased about it, as his supercilious tone and his failure to remember Buttle's correct name told him. 'This is highly unusual and inconvenient,' the chief steward repeated his complaint from earlier this evening on having been asked to assist in the first place, and he now demanded to know: 'How long must I remain here playing gaoler?'

Until we get to bloody Broome, Frank Buttle wanted to say, but he could only reasonably ask: 'Two hours for the time being would be appreciated – and another couple in the morning, if it can be managed, by you or anyone else of senior rank who might be available, and only until we're at sea again.' For then, he needn't keep such a close eye on Finlay McFarland, not until they were preparing to dock in Broome.

For now, he was bounding up the companionway, up two decks to McFarland's door. It was almost ten pm and, once there, he looked down and saw the note was gone from where it had been, sticking out under the door. Inside, through the half-open louvres he could see the bedside lamp was on. The light was poor, but he saw the back of the man, leaning over something as he sat on the edge of the bed; he looked as if he was perhaps writing, the way his elbow moved. Buttle didn't care what he was doing, so long as he was there. Settling in for the night: good.

He moved back out of the corridor and onto the promenade, stood there by the cabin window for about ten minutes, attempting to smoke a cigarette as the wind charged around him, spotting rain, determined to put it out. He saw the light go off in the cabin; heard the faint creak of springs as the bloke lay down on his bed. Buttle exhaled with satisfaction, and with a confirmation of his plans.

First: get something to eat – he was just about starving, having missed dinner in all this piddling around. As for McFarland, Frank Buttle had decided he was going to arrest him off his own bat, just as they docked in Broome in about thirty-six hours or so. He was now satisfied beyond a doubt that this bloke was the crook involved in the New South Wales property scam – he was Finlay McFarland. Buttle was convinced he had seen the proof of it on that note; he was confident that he could slap the cuffs on and prevail. To be extra sure, he'd have him for impersonating a retired naval officer, and for attempting to obtain some advantage from Miss Irene Everley by deception as well – and that last would be no lie, as Miss Everley was, by any interpretation, most certainly being had. It would bring her little humiliation to admit to it once all the other charges were laid out, either; only justice done. He'd make every one of those charges stick, too: once he sent word up to Hal Everley, in Derby, the whole lot would stick like shit to a sheep's arse. And in turn Frank Buttle would stick this to the Western Australian Police Force – from the little Hedland constable who'd spoken to him this afternoon as if he were the hired help, right up to the super at Broome. Then he'd say see you later to the whole bloody lot of them.

MIYA

Jarrod Neath knew the consequences of being caught selling snide, that it would, at best, ruin his career, and at worst see him sent to prison not only for trading in stolen goods, but for his embezzlement of bank funds that had largely paid for this venture. He was perhaps the coolest and most clear-thinking of the thieves; he did not allow the grim facts of failure to unsteady his nerve. Whether his clarity of mind came via hubris or stupidity, I don't know, but he believed, wholly believed, he would succeed in this and reap a profit of £14,063 by night's end. If he could somehow have flown away from Port Hedland that night unnoticed, he would have kept what he'd stolen from the bank, too.

He took the black box from the inside pocket of his suit coat and held me there in his right hand as Abraham Davis continued with the pleasantries: 'Would you like a cigar?'

'Cigar? No, thank you, Abe,' Neath replied, oblivious to the grimace that twitched across the face of Abraham Davis. But I noticed it; I could see Abraham Davis in his entirety, now that he was so near, his soul a large, plump orb of golden light – and I could feel how he hated being called Abe, especially by this man, to whom he was friendly and respectful, but for whom he felt little friendship or respect.

'I've had a spot of asthma,' Neath explained, lying, affecting a little cough. He wanted to get away as quickly as possible once the deal was done; the last thing he wanted was a chat over a cigar.

'Yes, it's late.' Abraham Davis was relieved at the refusal; the last thing he wanted was for Neath to hang about. 'It's far too late to be doing business at all,' he said. 'Let me see this Rosy of yours.'

'Ah yes, here we are.' Neath raised me up to the harsh white light of the electric lamp overhead and even before he lifted the lid of the box, my own light burst from me with my song.

I sang into Abraham's heart. I caressed every corner of his mind with my desire. And I cried for him as I sang, because I knew, for all his vacillation up until this point, he would not resist me anymore.

'Oh,' was the only sound he could utter when he saw me. 'Oh.'

He could see I was worth at least the £25,000 he had thought to sell me on for – and possibly much more. He was already revising his plans. The buyer he had in mind, in New York – a man called Hyram Resnick – would want this pink pearl at just about any price; he in turn would sell it on to a stock-market millionaire who would want me not only for my beauty, but for my muddied, mysterious provenance – he might get as much as half a million for me, in US dollars. I was the largest and the rosiest pearl Abraham Davis had ever seen. Within a blink, he had decided that he would cut his season short in Broome, make his way to the United States as soon as possible. His only quandary was whether or not he should ask the young woman, Margaret Carson, to accompany him, perhaps as his secretary – a sweet charade. Evans, his actual secretary, could remain here, to look after his affairs. He was already reaching for the case that contained his cash, the package of £20,000 in fifty-pound notes he had withdrawn for this purpose, still wrapped in its tissue paper from the bank.

Neath watched the pearler unlock the case, noted the slight tremble of excitement in the man's hands, and for a moment he wondered if he should have asked Davis for an even higher price. He called himself away from that, though, as a thought come too late, and instead imagined his own visit to the travel-booking agency, requesting passage to the Continent, to the French Riviera, the Côte d'Azur, where he would finally begin leading the life he had always believed he was entitled to – aperitif in one hand, and a piece of female flesh in the other.

But a man as wise and well-practised at his trade as Abraham Davis had to hesitate a moment to wonder, even over my siren song.

With his hand on the package of bank notes, he asked Neath: 'Tell me, who is the dealer? We are in total confidence here. Tell me.'

Abraham Davis did not want some criminal syndicate chasing after him; he had to know, as devious as this deal remained, that he would not encounter any unmanageable surprises. He could barely believe he was doing this at all. Dealing in snide. What was he thinking?

I scattered his thoughts again with my pleas for him to grasp me, to hold me in his hand, to feel my power, so that he could barely hear Neath's explanation.

'Don't worry,' Neath said. 'It's someone we both know. Someone wanting to pass on the hot potato as efficiently as possible. Someone with as much at stake as you.'

Abraham Davis nodded. He would have believed anything at that moment. There was only one other dealer in the Nor'-West with as much at stake, and that was Sydney Piggot himself, his only real business rival. He took the money from the case and placed it on the table, pushing it towards Neath.

The banker placed the black box on the table, too, pushing me towards Abraham Davis.

Mr Davis, oh how I cried for him. His apprehension and regret were at one with mine.

But the deal was done. Neath was bending down to his own case that lay on the floor beside the table. The locks snapped open, and then closed, and Neath was standing to leave, hand outstretched for the final shake. The curse would be broken soon, and I would be returned to the sea, the place where I belonged.

*

From where I remained for the moment on the table in that cabin, I followed the footsteps of Jarrod Neath back out into the night, back along the jetty and into the town, where I searched all around him and sang to the first angry man I could find.

It was a man whose name I would never learn, but whose anger I could see as a flame writhing in the darkness. A flame of righteous anger: his cousin, a young fellow, had been taken by the police for a crime he had not committed. This cousin, whose name he did not tell me either then, had been accused of spearing and killing a steer, but he had been nowhere near the cattle of his accuser; he'd been with a girl twenty miles away, his new wife, sharing a camp with her for the very first time – he wouldn't have been after anything but her. His accuser had made it up: another lie to get the police to come out and clear them off the land along the river, to clear them off further and further away from their own country. The police and the cattlemen would not stop until they had pushed them all onto the reserves at a place called Sunday Island, under the lash of the Church – just another kind of gaol.

This man knew nothing of me, nor of pearls, nor of money, but he could hear my song, he could feel it rising up through the soles of his feet, such was the strength of my voice now; such was the strength of his anger, too. I sang to that anger as the banker, Jarrod Neath, walked towards the customs sheds across from the jetty, where the man stood waiting, watching by the closed and bolted doors. Neath's home lay only half a mile away, a commodious weatherboard bungalow, for all that it appeared austere from the outside, as everything did in Port Hedland: why bother with fancy verandahs and rose gardens when the yearly visiting cyclonic winds would only rip them away? Neath hated Port Hedland, every day, he hated it now in the pitch dark, despite all it had given him. He did not have the slightest gratitude for the fact that a man such as he – son of a carpenter from Albany – could not have risen so high in his profession without this place; he was not grateful for the fact that he might have retired in a few years' time to a pleasant cottage in Perth, one with a waterside view. That was not good enough for him. These were among his final thoughts as he quickened his pace towards what he believed he deserved in his future.

He did not see or hear his assailant begin to follow him, as he passed by the rear of the Pier Hotel and the shipping agent that lay beyond it – Smith & Timms, the travel-booking office he believed he'd be walking into tomorrow as soon as they were open for business. He barely finished this thought. He felt only the sudden pressure under his chin, around his throat; the knee in his back; he heard the sharp crack of cartilage and bone as his neck snapped.

This was his end; he would breathe on for a few hours there where he slumped to the sand, but he did not wake again.

The angry man dragged Neath into the lane between the shipping agent's and the hotel; he robbed him of his watch there, but was disturbed before he could search for a wallet or pick up the case. The wind this night, strengthening again, blew the loose tin lid off the small brick incinerator at the back of the hotel, smashing it onto the wall of the shipping agent's, and startling the man, causing him to run, tripping over the case as he made his way, as fast as he could, a dark shape disappearing into the ever-gathering dark. The air crackled and cooled again as I continued to call it to me across the ocean; the camels that sat waiting for tomorrow's journey inland knew what was coming; they could smell the distant rain. And so could the angry man. I saw his fears for his cousin as he ran; he was as concerned for what the storm might bring as he was for what the experience of prison would do to him. He feared that his cousin – so young and only just become fully a man – was destined to be broken one way or another. As he ran, in grief he gave me the young fellow's name, and it came as a blow: Warlitj.

At last I saw: the silent one in chains on the ship, it was Warlitj – the boy who first found me. The boy who knew me. The only one who would have saved me from this fate if he could have done. This was a tragedy I could not have foreseen; and though I wailed in my own horror at it, there was nothing I could do to remove Warlitj from that ship. Who could I sing to for that? His gaoler?

Justice had been so complete for Neath. His body would be discovered in the morning when the office of Smith & Timms opened at ten, all presuming the death accidental, garrotted by a flying incinerator lid, and the following day taken as some sort of divine retribution when the bank discovered his embezzlement, while the case containing the £20,000 would sit undiscovered for several years under the footings behind the front step of the shipping agent, a mystery forever, the money being eventually absorbed into state revenue. All so neat that all was lost; and all so well deserved.

But for Warlitj. How I howled in rage for Warlitj. I searched and searched to find a way that I might save him from what I was about to do.

At that moment, back in the cabin on the ship, Abraham Davis took the black box from the table with the intention of locking me into his case, and into the purser's safe. I howled so furiously then, he could not have heard me more clearly.

Hold me! I begged him. *Keep me near!*

And he did.

He took me out of the box and told me: 'Yes, I must keep you close.'

He took his suit coat from the wardrobe and placed me inside the long, narrow pocket that was sewn into the silk lining, a pocket he'd had made in all of his business suits, for incidental purchases, such as this. It was inconspicuous and unusual: it was thief-proof.

It was irrelevant now; it was simply where I needed to be. I couldn't be locked in the safe – that safe, I could see, was watertight. And if I was going to make any attempt to save Warlitj, I had to be in the water with him, I had to be able to get to him – somehow. I couldn't quite see how yet, but I knew my power would only increase again, by some magnitude, as soon as the water surrounded me. Whatever happened, I would try.

'Yes,' Mr Davis said to me, patting the pocket, checking I had slipped securely to the bottom of it, before closing me into the wardrobe, in that suit coat. 'I will forget about you until we reach Broome. I will decide what to do with you then.'

I saw that he was not so tempted by riches now. He was a rich man but not a greedy one. He did not want to profit from a crime. I saw that he still wondered if he might keep me for Miss Carson, for some day in the future, when legends about me might be forgotten or cleansed of death in some trick of tale-telling. He wondered if he might give me to his daughter, Dorothy, instead; perhaps for her twenty-first birthday – that was only four years away. Perhaps for her wedding one day.

In one distressing moment, he almost changed course completely. He had recently invested in a cattle property inland at Marble Bar and thought he might ask Miss Carson in the morning if she would like to come out on the train with him to look over the land, stay for a week or two there, until the next steamer north, prolong their time together; Evans could be their chaperone.

No! I might have blasted the door from the wardrobe with my fear that he would leave this ship – with me. *No!* And then I did something truly wicked to prevent it. I whispered into his soul: *She will never convert to your religion, Abraham. Stop wasting your time, making a fool of yourself.*

He frowned in confusion at the lie. But it worked. It was too easy to make him doubt her. It was too easy to manipulate him, to ransom his heart.

He was a good man, Abraham Davis; I wished I could have saved him, too.

*

There was only one other moment of apprehension for me. In the morning, early, as preparations were being made to depart for Broome, the captain of the *Koombana*, Tom Allen, left the ship to consult with the captain of the *Bullarra*, Harry Upjohn, about the increasingly bad weather. I watched Tom Allen walk along the jetty to the other steamship, as I watched all so very carefully that day.

'What do you think?' Tom Allen asked Upjohn, but he was really asking himself and the clouds that shifted restlessly across the sky, layer over layer and swiftly now as I continued to call and gather them across the ocean. It looked to Tom Allen like the forewarning of a hurricane, this sky, and he was worried at the strength of the tide, too, being just about on the autumnal equinox, how that might play with the swell, but he knew himself to be a sometimes overly cautious fellow, and the subject of a few jibes over the years because of it. This was why he was master of the *Koombana*, the Adelaide Steamship Company's most prestigious vessel, though.

Harry Upjohn smiled slowly, sensing his colleague's concern. 'Bit late in the year for a cyclone, isn't it, Tom?'

'Yes.' Tom Allen smiled in return at his more easy-going counterpart. This was why Harry Upjohn was master of the *Bullarra*, the Adelaide Steamship Company's best old and rusting hulk. She was heading south with mostly cattle, the last of which were about to be boarded now.

And that thought gave Tom Allen further cause to consider the risks that might lie ahead. The *Koombana* was carrying barely any cargo but the mail, which made the ship sit high in the water – that was the whole idea of the *Koombana*'s design, with her ballast at the barest minimum, that she would sit a little high, so that she could get through shallow harbours like this one with greater ease, get out over the sandbar at the entrance which had caught even her before, on a mean tide – but it also meant that she was top heavy in high seas and heavy storms, most especially with so little weight in her. It was all right for the *Bullarra* – nothing would knock that tough old lady down. But the *Koombana* ...

Tom Allen thought perhaps it would be better to delay his departure by one day and shelter here instead.

No! I cried out to rattle the deck rails, but Tom Allen could only hear the wind as it shrieked past his ears. He had no knowledge of my existence, nor the slightest bit of interest in any business but his shipboard responsibilities, no desire for anything but the work at hand. I could not seem to make him hear anything from within, no matter how I tried.

But then luck once again intervened.

'You're not worried are you?' Harry Upjohn winked at Tom Allen, teasing him – only lightly, with some affection, but it was enough. The small challenge that lay in that question, the dare, the comradely competition between men, shot through the doubts of Captain Allen so that as he looked away, east over the town, I was able to force a break in the clouds, force the rising sun into his eyes, to cast those doubts completely to the wind.

'Worried?' Tom Allen replied with a chuckle, at himself as much as his colleague. 'Good heavens, no.'

The *Koombana* would push out of Port Hedland as scheduled; she would sail at ten-thirty am.

*

'Have you seen Irene anywhere?' Miss Carson was overcome with worry as she hurried back to the saloon. The ship's whistle had sounded; the propeller churned through the water, heaving the ship away from the jetty towards the harbour's entrance.

The woman called Suzette Leighton only looked sourly at Miss Carson, as if she had spoken to her improperly, as if she were a servant speaking rudely to her mistress.

'Suzette, I don't care in the least whatever it is you might think of me. I need to find Irene. Have you seen her?'

A wave of guilt rose and swelled all around Marg Carson: for presuming, all this time, that her friend had merely been getting on with her dissolute rendezvousing, and enjoying it perhaps too much, not bothering to make an appearance at dinner. Imagining that Irene had been sleeping in, while Marg herself sat in the dining room designing wedding bouquets in her mind over breakfast. Indulging herself, idly. Spending an hour at her toilette, attempting to make herself beautiful with powder and scent, for Mr Davis, for coffee at ten. And only then, when he'd asked her where Irene was, had she suddenly wondered, with alarm. She had rushed out to batter on the door of her friend's cabin, to search the bathrooms, the promenade, the second-class saloon where all manner of more interesting things often occurred. Irene, it seemed, was nowhere on the ship.

'Not with Mr Sinclair?' Suzette Leighton sneered, and turned her shoulder away, where she sat, alone, in one of the club chairs by the windows.

'Not with Mr Sinclair, no,' Marg Carson replied pointedly, warning Mrs Leighton against voicing any nasty thought.

But Mrs Suzette Leighton would voice it regardless. 'You know what they're up to, don't you?' she said, over her shoulder. 'They're probably still in bed. Are you so very loyal, or are you simply blind?'

Marg shook her head in quite another wonder at the woman but she did not respond.

'Miss Carson.' Mr Davis was at her side now, a little out of breath from his own rushing around. 'Mystery solved and I'm afraid it's not the best news.'

'What is it?' Every fear screeched through her before Mr Davis stilled her panic.

'Miss Everley, it appears, has met with something of an accident,' he explained. 'Don't be too concerned – I'm assured she's all right, but unfit for travel and being held over at the hospital for a day or two, having hit her head somehow outside the Esplanade Hotel, knocked herself out, poor dear girl. Harris, the purser, sends his apologies for not informing you sooner. It seems we've all been a little preoccupied, hm?'

'Oh.' Marg Carson felt the wash of relief go straight to her knees. This certainly wasn't the first time her wayward charge had run into such trouble, just another minor mishap after one gin too many. Irene had given herself the most hideous black eye only two months ago hitting the doorknob in their rooms at the Grand in Melbourne, misjudging the distance, tipsy. Of course, that's all it was: she's only resumed drinking: a couple of martinis at the Esplanade Hotel, as was her usual custom. But this relief was followed by a sigh of annoyance at the inconvenience it presented: Marg would have to get off the ship in Broome and wait for another, to go back for her. She was making a list of everything else that would need to be done – a telegram sent on to Mr Everley, belongings gathered and accommodations arranged – when Mr Davis spoke again, apparently having read her mind.

'You might consider stopping at De Vahl.' He smiled a little mischievously over his spectacles, and added: 'She's well staffed. Your reputation is safe with me.'

He dared this now, and all too late.

So close between them I lay, there in his pocket, listening as they laughed, perhaps a little too loudly, and watching as Marg Carson looked down at Suzette Leighton, hoping she'd heard them; hoping she'd spread some of her awful gossip as well, for Marg had never had anything like that said about her.

She looked out through the windows, smiling, and she couldn't see the storm at all.

*

One lone man stood at the rail outside: the policeman, Corporal Buttle. He waited on the promenade deck for the one called Finlay McFarland to emerge – a man who meant nothing to me, except that he might yet have caused the ship to return to dock.

Buttle deliberated what to do – arrest him now and take him down below with the other prisoners, or wait until tomorrow when they arrived in Broome? Instinct told him not to trust his luck, to make a move now, belt down the door of the cabin if need be; but caution told him to wait – to not risk alarming passengers and crew with what might well be a dramatic apprehension. He decided to give it half an hour longer, until eleven-thirty, when he was due to return below himself.

The *Koombana* shuddered, meeting the rough and racing ocean waters beyond the harbour; and the wind roared around him as he looked back at Port Hedland. Odd, he thought on seeing the harbour so empty of luggers; there were usually two or three dozen anchored all around it at any one time. Only the *Bullarra* was there, waiting to follow them out, or so it seemed to him. He couldn't see from where he stood that all the pearling schooners were sheltering deep inside the fingers of Stingray Creek at the back of the harbour on this high tide. The skippers of these smaller vessels were not taking any chances with the weather: they knew what was coming; they knew they were in for a great blow.

So did Warlitj. My light flew back to him, again and again, where he sat in the darkness of the cattle stalls, chained to the other prisoners. For all that he could not see me, he knew the storm was almost upon them, he could feel it, but he was now gone to a place past fear. He was so consumed by defeat his soul had all but returned to the universal pool of light from which we all come and to which we all return; he was returning to his true home, he believed, to the spirit world of his ancestors. I wished he could see me and know me as he had known me once, all those years ago, but I could not get through to him. I was still yet in the pocket of Abraham Davis. I wished I could tell Warlitj to wake from his deathly dream, to be ready for me, for his freedom, here on earth. I sang to him as best I could; I searched for a way into his thoughts to let him know that I would try to reach him in the storm, but it was no good.

I glimpsed only the questing soul of that man called Finlay McFarland. He must have been somewhere near, but where I could not have cared – I didn't have the time nor the need to seek him.

But in that glimpse, I saw he was no more a thief than Warlitj; I sensed the chains that held him, too; I sensed the urgency of his love for the woman, Irene. But there was nothing I could do for him.

It was time now for my return. I gathered in all my light, and I began to sing, to shriek and soar, as I had never done before.

*

The sea became the air, the rain so heavy and the waves so high, while the heat within me screamed with such ferocity, I felt this power might destroy me, too, before the ship capsized. I was inside the ship; I was all around the ship; I watched it rolling starboard first before it began to sink. I watched all souls upon it die.

I felt the final distress call from the wireless fracture and scatter in the gale towards nowhere but obliteration. I saw the young operator desperately tapping out the message, a boy of nineteen, crying out for his mother as the water rose around him. I saw Hedley Harris shielding the stewardess, Mrs Freer, as the windows of the lower saloon exploded with the force. I saw them all, and I mourned them all, each death a shard of deepest regret, even as I screamed yet more fiercely for the water to come for me.

I was sure my shell would crack in two. Shatter into grains of sand. I was almost fearful of what the water would do to me once it came. How I might expand. What my power would do. For I knew this change was coming: I could see it as a white-hot blast.

Until, at last, it came, not with pain, but in a startling rush, a cool rush of peace amid the crashing of the storm, such a peace that I could hear no other sound but the beating of one heart: the heart that belonged to Warlitj. Chained against the back of that cattle stall, he was held up from the water. Only just. He was still alive.

I knew nothing of time, but that I had so little of it left to me to reach him. Through the cool I sent my light with all my force, with all my concentration, towards him as a stream, which became a blade, which became a needle, a white-hot needle that rent its way through the ship, through iron and steel and timber, to thread around the heavy noose that held him. I sliced through every chain and then I held him in a tight warm ball of air as I thrust him through the listing ship, and through the sea. The water gushed around him but did not touch him, and as we flew this way, he told me that the meaning of his name, his true name, was Eagle, and he prayed that he would live; he prayed that the spirits who had him in their grasp would be kind.

I brought him back to the air beyond the now fading edges of the cyclone, and I laid him on a door that had been ripped from the upper saloon. He breathed there in the sudden stillness, and he saw what had happened. He saw that he was free. Through the haze of cloud and spray that yet hung across the sky he could just discern the silver gulls that circled above land not very far away; their cries of irritation at the storm that had swept across their cliff top; their tiny red-dot beaks. Warlitj could easily swim to shore from here, back to his family, back to his young wife, and that is what he did.

My power then began to fade, too, and with the last of it, I blew the weakening storm south, over the *Bullarra*, over the island called Balla Balla, and from there into the desert, along the creeks and rivers, flooding and stretching into the Pilbara, as far as I could reach.

And then I left. I floated free from Mr Davis, Abraham, his arms still held in protective embrace, although Miss Carson had gone from him, too. I suppose they recognised each other in the pool when next they met; I hope so.

I sailed from the wreck and settled back into the shallows below the reef. Here. Where I was born, and where I remain. At last, I was brought home.

IRENE

'Tigs darling, please.' My sister Marie is taking a turn at attempting to reassure me. 'There's nothing you could have done. There's nothing you can do.'

Oceanna has daily said the same; Derek and Gus, their husbands, too; and Dad. It's not my fault. Merely an accident of fate. A random loss of footing; falling. Beyond reason.

The ship is yet to be found.

I snap at Marie: 'Of course there's nothing I could have done – do I look like God?'

'You look terrible,' Marie snaps back and returns to the children in the drawing room.

They'll all leave soon, go back to their bungalows that lie not far enough away inside this tiny colony of Everley. I wish they'd stay away and forget I exist at all. Leave me to sit here in my sitting room staring out at nothing until nothing comes for me. I'd start drinking to hasten it, if I could stomach the smell.

I return to the newspapers instead, obsessively hunting for information, for clues, re-reading any mention over and over, and snatching at anything new. I don't remember the cyclone, except for the skull-crunching headache I had, which had me wanting to tear the shutters off the hospital window to stop the banging. It didn't hit Heddy very hard, anyway; although some unlucky chap was killed by a flying incinerator lid, barely a window was cracked throughout the town, and all I thought for the first few days was how embarrassing and annoying it was that the ship had left without me. Until it failed to arrive in Broome.

It's been missing for over a month now. Six weeks and two days. Today is the third of May.

No-one is coming home. Marg. Mr Davis.

Fin.

I can't bear to even think of him. His face.

He can't have vanished into the sea. I dive back into my pile of *West Australians*, Saturday *Truth*s and Perth *Daily*s that get into Derby always at least a fortnight after any fact that might be found among the endless and inane gossip. I pore over Dad's copies of the *Pilbara News*, which he only gets to keep abreast of things on the goldfields, and an eye on the price per ounce.

The timing of it all seems too uncanny to believe. By all calculations and speculations, the *Koombana* left Port Hedland at ten-thirty am, and was last seen by the captain of the *Bullarra* about an hour later as he, too, came out of the harbour, heading south, while the *Koombana* continued north. The cyclone was moving in a south-easterly direction, hitting the *Bullarra* a few hours later – which can only mean that, if it did hit the *Koombana*, it must have hit her barely off the coast. How could Captain Allen, rigorously serious and sensible Tom Allen, have run his ship right into the path of a cyclone?

And if that's what happened, where is the ship? If she ran aground on reef or rocks, where is the wreck?

Where are the survivors?

I see them waving from an island yet to be discovered. I will somehow discover it. I will find them, through the mist.

The captain of the *Bullarra*, Harry Upjohn, said the storm came on so quickly, it was like nothing he'd ever seen. He said the ocean foam was flung about like whirling snow and that a great spiral of cloud descended right down to the water so that nothing could be seen at all.

I have mad waking dreams that the ship was sucked into the sky by the vortex.

The island is in the sky. On a cloud.

Odd pieces of flotsam have appeared. Off the island of Bedout, sixty miles north of Heddy, a cushion from a sofa was found, but it's not described in any of the papers – is it violet moquette? A bag of empty bottles was seen drifting cryptically nearby; a section of ceiling somewhere else – but was it decorated with gold stars?

Saloon or dining room? Who knows? A door was found by a lugger searching off Rowley Shoals in the Timor Sea, five hundred miles away – a lugger called, by some sick irony, the *Gorgon*. The door is oak-panelled, polished, fingerplate ornamented with a Grecian urn. It can only be presumed to have come from the *Koombana*.

No. You can't believe what you read in the papers – two weeks overdue and at least half made up.

Stories abound and no amount of repeating any of them will ever make them truth. Monstrous seas flooded the ship through the main deck, through the cattle stalls, to sink her, says one theory. Another says the lighthouse at Bedout had not been in operation, perhaps causing Captain Allen to misjudge the ship's distance from the rocks in the hours after the storm had passed – in broad daylight. Really? Captain Allen would be so stupid? Drunk? Yet another supposes that her engine became inexplicably disabled, and the storm by tragic coincidence then drove her somewhere over deep water and made her founder there, to so completely disappear. And another still says that Captain Allen made some wrong decision against the wind, causing the ship to heel over, lose its ballast and capsize. They'll have to blame him somehow, for the insurance, Dad said with mild and unsurprised disgust. Blame the dead captain and the mute, inscrutable witness that is the sea.

No-one at the Adelaide Steamship Company will take any responsibility if they can help it. They don't know anything. They don't even know how many were on board. One hundred and forty passengers? One hundred and fifty? Every passenger list is different, and not one of them has Marg listed. Who made that spectacular clerical error? There's no record of Fin, either. Nor Suzette Leighton, nor her maid. I've drawn up lists of the lists. Only Mr Davis appears on them all. And me: Irene Everley. Presumed lost.

An empty lifebelt wandering lonely on the waves.

An indecipherable jumble of Morse code picked up in the Strait of Bali: *This is the Koombana. We are ...*

Gone. The purser, lovely Mr Harris. The Skamp sisters, Gennie and Alice. Mrs Freer, the stewardess – she always took such good care with my laundry, and I never knew her name was Anastasia. Mr Spark, who ran the grog shop in town. All gone but for their names in black and white, there, in this list or that. The officers. The cooks. The stewards. The team of firemen who stoked the engine – men I never thought of, not really, except when they all went on strike last year and delayed the ship. They are all vanished. They are perished.

Corporal Buttle, too, and it's only now – here in this inescapable swash of loss upon loss – that I remember he was the one who came out to Everley when Mum died; he rode the fifty miles from Derby flat out, and even still managed to look as if he'd shined his shoes especially. That's why I never liked to see him, that's why I never liked him near: because I hate remembering ...

I hate remembering what I might have done and didn't; couldn't. But could I have?

Memory is so strange; stranger than facts; stranger than fiction. Mr Davis lives happily ever after and eternally with Marg in 'Purple Daze', as Ishmael of the *Peapod* and Perle de le Prix. I can't read that copy. I never will.

I hate that I ever wrote anything. I hate that I ever laughed.

I imagine a Gorgon, enraged, smashing her fists through the clouds, her head full of snakes all striking blindly at the mist, striking out at unreachable, uncaring Poseidon. Because I am. I make no sound, I hardly move, but rage is all I am.

*

Something other than rage descends upon me when the next bundle of newsprint arrives from Derby. The paper is dated April 17th – sixteen days ago – and screams from the world-affairs columns of page seven:

OCEAN DISASTER
TITANIC SUNK
ENORMOUS LOSS

London, April 16

Reports received from the American side of the Atlantic state that the mammoth White Star liner Titanic, *which struck an iceberg off Newfoundland on Sunday night, sank on Monday morning between Sable Island and Cape Race, in water two miles deep.*

The SS. Carpathia, now on her way to New York, picked up life-boats containing 866 of the Titanic's passengers. Mostly women, they include Mrs Jacob Astor, the Countess of Rothes, Mr. J.B. Ismay (managing director of the White Star Line), Sir Cosmo Gordon, and Mr Bahr (the well-known tennis player).

The officials of the White Star Line now believe that 1,500 of the Titanic's passengers have been drowned. The details of the disaster and of the rescue operations are, however, meagre and contradictory.

GIGANTIC FIGURES

The lost vessel cost £1,250,000, and her hull and cargo were insured for £2,350,000. Reinsurances were effected on Monday at 50 guineas per cent. The liner carried £1,000,000 worth of diamonds and £500,000 worth of pearls.

THE ICEFIELDS

Various liners recently encountered an icefield 100 miles long and 35 miles broad off the Newfoundland Grand Banks. Veteran Atlantic voyagers' state that they have never before seen ice in such great bulk so far south as it is at present in the North Atlantic. The bergs are mostly without tops. They are merely awash, and it is difficult to discern them.

'What is it, my girl?' Dad says behind me. He's come in with my cup of tea, because he is my wonderful father, who is not out on the station wilds bringing in bull calves with Gus and Derek, because he's looking after me, watching over me, anxiously, but for a moment I can't even grunt at him. I'm not sure if I've gone completely mad. The *Titanic* has sunk?

Ten times the size of *Koombana*, it was supposed to be unsinkable. I am having another waking dream, I suppose, only the steam rising from my teacup seems real enough. And the black-and-white facts are too believable, meagre and contradictory as they may be: first class on the transatlantic leviathan has managed to have itself rescued, while steerage has been jettisoned, and the generous terms of insurance have made the wholesale tragedy somehow worthwhile.

But other facts loom out of the lines like harbingers of worse to come: pearls, half a million pounds' worth, colliding with a submerged iceberg, the likes of which no-one has seen before. Marg was right: some kind of curse lurks beyond the surface of things here, as if nature is trying to speak to us. Trying to shake us, from all our lies, our greed, our lust.

I stand abruptly and the teacup rattles in its saucer on the table.

Something cracks and falls away, deep inside me.

'My girl – Irene – what's the matter?' Dad's large, rough hand on my shoulder; he's so very worried about me.

I turn to him and look into his eyes, kind green eyes in his rough, old face of tanned and well-worn buffalo hide, and I tell him: 'I'm so sorry.' Because as yet, that is all I can say.

'Sorry?' He is confused, and always ready to defend me. 'You don't have anything to be sorry for, my tiger.'

But I do. I am the tiger; I have lived as if the world is mine to devour. I feel as if my wickedness, my selfish weaknesses have wrecked the world, however small my part might be in this catastrophe. Shame strangles my need to explain. 'Dad, I …'

'What is it, Irene?' I am terrifying my poor father; he is not frightened of anything, except that I might leave him as Mum did.

But I am not my mother: cold, dead, lying there on her bed like wretched, mad Ophelia. A different anger flares: how dare she wreck me as she did, in this house – right here, across the hall. How dare she use her life that way – to curse me.

Some truth bursts from me; the truth I came home to tell my father in the first place: 'Dad, you know I'll never marry, don't you. You know I'll never have any children.'

'What's that?' He is even more confused, and why wouldn't he be? I can hardly follow my thoughts, either. He says, so gently, so badly wanting to repair me: 'Now, now, don't go making any big decisions when you're upset, love. Wait until Marcus gets here, you'll feel better when he's here. That's it – I'm going to send off for him today, tell him to get here as quick as he can.'

'No, please.' I have refused this since arriving home a month ago, as I have refused all company, but I say it with some urgency here. 'Marksy and I are not going to be married. Please, hear me. We never intended to go through with it. I've been lying all this —'

'Has he mucked you about?' Dad squares his shoulders at the idea; he can't quite hear what I'm saying, or won't, and I would laugh at him if I could. My wonderful father, my dear Old Hal, is so very uncomplicated: of course, whatever has happened, it must all be anyone else's fault but mine; it must be Marksy's fault. He waves his hand dismissively, as if he's rejecting a bull at the yards. 'Plenty better than him out there, don't you worry. We'll get you another bloke, you'll see.'

'Dad, please. Listen to me,' I tell him as plainly as I can. 'I don't want another bloke.'

'What's that?' Dad rubs his forehead.

The blackest of my grief threatens to overwhelm me: the one I wanted is gone. He's on the island in the clouds, a thousand dreams away. I don't even know if he was ever real at all. I was not made to love or be loved.

'What do you want if you don't want to get married?' Dad asks me, because he can't possibly imagine what I might do, apart from going to Melbourne to shop, and Adelaide to catch up with chums.

I don't know if it's real anymore, either, but I tell him, finally, what I had most been longing to: 'I want to write.'

A desire smashed upon the rocks somewhere, but it's the only thing I have that I might begin to make something from, the only thing I might salvage, pay my debts with: the truth. Spend the rest of my life seeking it.

'Write?' This makes as much sense to Dad as my prior studies in Modern European History. Why would anyone want to do that?

'I want to be a writer.' I change the words around, trying to make sense of them myself. 'Write things.'

'What things?' He's only more uncomprehending; and the question tears through me with its echo: Fin looking up from unlacing his shoes: *What things?*

'I don't know.' I can only answer with the truth's vast, brass-bottomed paradox. 'I want to write about all the things I don't know.'

'You can write whatever you like, love.' Dad frowns; he wants to understand. 'Nothing stopping you, is there?'

'I can't write here,' I begin the worst of this confession to him. 'No-one would ever give me a job as a proper journalist or —'

'I'll get you the bleeding job,' Dad swears, ready to spring to the challenge. 'Where's the job – who's the feller? I'll speak to him.'

'Dad,' I finish the worst of this confession. 'I have to leave. There's nothing for me to write about here. I need ...' I need to run from the truths at my feet even as I'm seeking others; I need to break your heart. 'Dad, what I really need is to go abroad.'

In his frown I see his fears returned.

I tell him: 'I want to go to London.' Because I refuse to be frightened myself anymore. I'll be all right. I won't be too alone. We have several skerricks of family in England, in particular a cousin that Dad still corresponds closely with – his cousin Joe, in Kent, dairy farmer. This was always my original thought and most slimly sketched itinerary: London, Dover, ferry trip to Calais, Paris – and then everywhere else. Alone. So alone now. 'Please,' I beg him with my own heartbreak.

'Tiger.' He shakes his head, looks out of the window across his red-dust realm, across all his ambitions fulfilled, this rich slice of West Kimberley big-sky desert edge. 'It's too far away.'

'Please.' The entreaty rises from me as a demand, harsh and threatening: let me go or I will leave you anyway. I will die here.

'Well, I suppose ...' He has heard me, somehow. He looks me over with his sad and worried eyes, making a reluctant but necessary deal. 'Maybe it won't do you any harm, see what the fuss is all about. You'll be back after your first winter over there – that's my money.'

That's your money gone, and I think we both know it.

I let my forehead fall against his chest, with my thanks, and with my promise: I'll write only things that honour you from now on; his arms enfold me, and at last I feel their warmth. I am alive. I did survive. I am here. I can feel my feet inside my shoes. Truly.

'Aunty Tigsy! Aunty Tigsy!' A niece skitters in from down the hall. It's Katie, belonging to Oceanna; she's five and her head is a mad mess of golden ringlets. I've seen her almost every day since coming home, but it feels as if I'm seeing her for the first time, ever: darting right for me. 'Help me!' she yells out across my sitting room, my private mausoleum, wild with laughter: it's only big brother Rupe chasing her from house to house, possibly intent on some form of torture, making her forget that Aunty Tigsy is not to be disturbed.

'Children, please!' Mrs Riordan, the housekeeper, comes chasing after them with a feather duster.

But I have already gathered Katie up into my arms, and I have nestled her there, to breathe in her scent of warm, small girl. And I have begun to cry: I can't force it away any longer. I hold this little girl to me and I cry.

She pats me, on the back of my neck, so softly; she tells me, playing mother: 'It's all right, Tigsy. There, there, it's all right.'

And it is. Or it will be. Life goes on, doesn't it?

*

In the dawn, I ride out to the big waterhole that lies two miles east of Everley, towards the desert heart, practising my aloneness, practising goodbye. Two old boab trees stand by the edge of the water, their grey trunks swollen with contentment at being here, in their home. The wet-season storms have been kind in this place: the reeds are thick and green against the coppery sand; the air is filled with frog song. Memories fill with children squealing, splashing in thrilled panic, as Dad pretends to be a crocodile, stalking up behind us.

Behind me, under the vaulting ledge of an outcrop, ancient faces watch everything: white, moon-round faces painted on the flame-red rock; they glow with the rising sun. I look around for black faces watching me, too, but none are today, or not that I can see. Dad's learned over the years that this place is sacred to them. A place they call Woongkurroo; while we call it Big Waterhole. They believe that the spirits of all children are born here in this pool; it's easy to imagine why: the way the water reflects the sky. The men come to the homestead to let Dad know when we should stay away, when they hold corroborees of some sort here.

Dad always lets them get on with their business, always makes sure they have what they need to get along, and in exchange they stay away from his stock. A gentlemen's agreement, of sorts; the price paid for swindled real estate. For peace. And there is peace here.

But the moon creatures stare at me now in this dawn like a cloud of ghosts: pearl-faced wraiths; Freckle feels it, too: she shivers and shakes her head. It's time for me to go.

*

'I'll miss you,' Marksy tells me as we amble arm in arm along Lovers Walk, under the cliff at Peppermint Grove, the last of home.

'Barely,' I reply. It's not as though we ever spent more than a few months of the year in each other's company, and besides, he has a new lover: someone called Darius Maxwell – Darius this, Darius that – an industrial chemist, met him at the yacht club. I'm disappointed I won't get to make a personal appraisal of him in Melbourne – this one seems serious – but my ship is only sailing one way, out of Fremantle, and on Tuesday week, in eleven days' time.

The cool August wind ruffles his dark hair: my Marksy, he really is unspeakably gorgeous, dazzling as the sun on the water behind him where he stands. Rugby-solid Michelangelo, he won't have too much trouble finding another decoy, or ruining several hundred other hearts, and I'd write all the truth of that, if it wouldn't put us both in prison.

He squeezes my hand. 'Please, promise me, if you need the slightest thing, you'll go straight to Jocelynn.' His sister, in Highgate, married to a Westminster civil servant, undersecretary to the Chancellor of the Exchequer; I've never met her. My stomach leaps over itself with an odd exhilaration as he assures me: 'Nothing will shock her. Really – she knows everything about me, about most things. You can trust her, with anything.'

I look south, back along Freshwater Bay, towards Mosman Park, and I am still a little shocked myself, at the life that has begun inside me. I'm going to have a baby, and I can't be entirely sure if it might belong to Stuart Wakefield, or …

It doesn't matter who the father is: the child will be mine, and I thoroughly deserve whatever it might bring, beginning with the first story I must write: the extraordinary one which will explain your existence to my father, once we're a fair way off shore. I laugh into the wind as I press my hand to my child, where it grows. How can I not laugh? Monthlies a no-show four in a row, but still it was such a surprise. Astonishing. I'd thought that perhaps my body was being strange at the shock of things. How I laughed at the Doctor when I had it very discreetly confirmed a week ago, told that, no, it's highly unlikely that the swelling of my belly is the result of too many walnut creams; I laughed all the way to Boan Brothers' corset department to purchase one of those ugly but necessary things with the laces down the sides – for tennis, I said to the prying eyebrow there. Yes, some of us are dealt the most unfair blows, and some of us get precisely what we had coming.

Just as grief comes fast over my laughter, for I know whose child this is. Vague and remiss as I have always been about these matters, even I am aware it's almost impossible that it could be anyone else's. And I know what odd exhilaration this is, too: that I might see his face again, one day soon, in the face of my child.

'God, Tigs.' Marksy holds me here on this slim strip of river beach until the rush of loss subsides. 'Are you sure you don't want me to come with you?' he asks me, as he's asked me a dozen times now.

'Don't be silly,' I tell him again. He can't suspend his career and his own love to follow me to London, although I wish he would; I wish I could ask him to, but I won't do that. This is my messy bed. I do what I do best: I lie. 'I'm stupidly hungry.'

We walk back up to the house and by the time we get there, I am actually hungry, and a little tired. My hand on the pale stone of the balustrade seems too small for the enormity of all that lies ahead, too weak with this weariness that comes from growing things inside us. Finally, I am grasping what I have wanted for so long: my escape from Retreat, from Australia, but I suddenly seem too small for it. I could curl up into my messy bed and stay there forever, after an anchovy sandwich with mayonnaise, and a sprinkling of cayenne.

'Oh, Miss Everley, that's good timing.' One of the maids, Gretchen, is at the top of the steps, brushing the cushions on the cane lounge here, cleaning them of salt and sand. 'The mail just came.' She pulls a couple of envelopes from her apron pocket, and I wish it was a sandwich. I wonder what they'd think of this in London: the maid handing me the mail to save her from bringing it in to me. She even flirts with Marksy: 'Nice out, Mr Densforth?'

I don't hear his reply. I'm looking at one of the letters, imagining that the neat and careful handwriting on it is neat and careful enough to be —

It won't be, but I tear the envelope open anyway, wanting it to be. I suppose I'll always want it to be.

FIN

Dear Irene,
I hope this letter finds you well. That doesn't seem an
adequate thing to say in the circumstances, but here we are.
At least, here I am, hoping that this letter finds you at all.

I've only recently discovered that you weren't on the
ship – it's been a time in hell thinking that you were. Your
name appeared in a paragraph on the Koombana, *in a copy*
of the Darwin Gazette, *weeks old by the time I came*
across it. It was only a brief mention, saying that, contrary
to reports, you had disembarked at Port Hedland and were
safe with your family. It was only by chance that I read it,
and when I did, I shed some tears of relief. To know that
you are alive, wherever you are – I can't describe what
happiness this brings me.

Why did you disembark at Port Hedland, Irene? I am not
a man given to religion or any other kind of mystical belief,
but I can only think some angel must have pulled you from
that ship.

Not so for me. Sneaking away in the night is my speciality.
Where do I begin? I'm in Singapore now, where I managed to
talk my way into a job with Dalgety & Co, as a cargo-
booking agent – so it wasn't difficult for me to obtain an
address for 'Everley' from your father's shipping account with
the firm. I don't know what or if you might think of me, if

my going from your life has brought sadness or relief. I don't know if you would have got my note telling you goodbye, apologising for my cowardice – did you find it under your cabin door? Is that why you left the ship? Were you angry, looking for me? Or did it only sink to the bottom of the sea? Whatever the case may be, I want you to know that I am as sorry today as I was then. I could not allow you to be associated with someone like me. I could only bring you embarrassment and pain – failure of every kind.

I don't expect a reply from you, nor do I want one. I only want you to know how happy I am that you are in the world, doing whatever it is you might be doing – at your typewriter, smoking a cigarette, chewing the end of a pencil, breathing. I think of you often, and I think of you only with the deepest affection and respect.

By early December, I will have left Singapore forTokyo, and a new post there, exporting silk handkerchiefs and teacups for sheepskins and barrels of beef, or whatever the present expansions of trade with Japan will entail. I've been very fortunate to have found this position, this fresh start. I've been fortunate most of all in having known you, even though we had too short a time together.

Be well, Irene Everley. I wish you the very best in your life.
Always,
James Finlay – and whoever else I must be to get on with my own.

MIYA

The warm sea clouds with other storms, and it clears, again and again, year after year, millennia after millennia. I drift with the tides and the currents, waiting for my next change, my next shape, beginning and beginning, always seeking to return to this place, this timeless seat of all creation and renewal, this sweet pool that we all share.

As you must inevitably return here, too, for you are no less eternal than the sea yourself, no less eternal than me. And yet we, all spirits trapped in form, clutch so desperately at now, at survival, when survival is as accidental as life itself. This is the enigma from which you are made. All that you see is an accident, cruel and beautiful, ephemeral and indelible, and every act of love is a prayer, a thread strung tight between hope and despair.

To walk upon that thread, that high, tight string of love, is the only road to the light there is, and to dare to fall from it, to plunge and scramble in the depths, is the only means by which you might ever find the light – the jewel – in you.

There is no other way of being.

There is no other power.

IRENE

'**M**r Finlay.'

There he is behind the outgoings counter at Dalgety's, tie crisply knotted, hair crisply trimmed, not a dot of perspiration on his brow despite the equatorial steam house I find him in, on this cloud island of Singapore. He is deep in conference with another man, discussing a shipment of Gippsland wool going on from here to Japan. I'm having some trouble breathing in the warm, wet air; remaining vertical might be a challenge, too, if it weren't for the thrill of my life holding me up.

I try again: 'Excuse me, Mr Finlay.'

He sees me at last, and doesn't trust the sight. 'I ... Ah ...' His face is caught in a contest between alarm and delight.

I tease him in front of his colleague: 'Yes, that's right. Thought you'd got away, did you?'

'Irene?' He still doesn't believe it, stepping around the side of the counter to test the truth.

'Yes,' I repeat. 'It's me. Irene. Thought you might like to see how very well I am in person. Aren't you pleased? Darling?'

I place my hand where my waist used to be, so that he can see more precisely what I am referring to. And there is plenty to see: I am rather larger than I was when I received his letter, twenty-five days ago; rather less neo-classically frocked than making a poor attempt to conceal the obvious. So large now I feel our child inside me, moving in its small sea there.

I watch Fin's hand touch mine and we are together again.

Here.

Oh, this love.

'What's that?' his colleague says from behind the counter. 'You never said you were married.'

'Didn't I?' Fin replies but he doesn't take his eyes from me. 'Well, now you know. I am. Apparently.'

He touches my face, the rush of all his questions reduced to one: 'How?'

But I can't tell him yet. All words are lost to me for this moment, too, as he holds me in this cluttered and sweaty shipping office.

The touch of his face against mine; I can't let him go for some time, as if he might disappear again if I do.

Oh, this love. This happy, happy love.

I shall always remember us here, inside its safest harbour.

*

I remember it now. Daily. Sometimes on the hour. I play our strokes of good fortune out one by one, to remind myself of their existence, capricious though luck might be.

It was only a fortnight after our reunion that we got the telegram from Marksy confirming that all police warrants against Fin had been torn up. It hadn't taken much detective work, and all up less than two months. Once the original partnership agreement with the convicted cheat, McElroy, was unearthed, together with the bank records of the real estate business and those belonging to Fin himself, it was clear that Fin had been as deceived as anyone – or so decided the New South Wales Chief Prosecutor, at least, who happens to be the father of one of Marksy's many chums, and by stunning small-country coincidence the brother of Dad's Sydney livestock agent. We were on our way to the port of Southampton by the time the file was closed and removed to a dusty cupboard. Money is a wonder when you're on the right side of it, isn't it?

Justice, on the other hand, is a more mercurial beast.

Eddie, our son, is nearly four now, and he is unmistakeably our son – so fair he is almost silver; the small-boy square of his face and his watchful eyes are his father's. Dad will always believe he was born in the June of 1913 rather than the previous December; a small-boy lie that distance can't unravel. He wouldn't believe it if he was told the truth, anyway – Dad can't remember my birthday, never mind any of his grandchildren's. He's far too pleased I'm married and breeding – with a 'decent ex-naval chap, twenty-four-carat character', so Marksy described Fin to Dad, another gentle bending of the truth as Marksy hasn't met Fin any more than Dad has – yet. A lie that's not really a lie at all: Dad will love him when he sees how much and why I love him, when they do finally meet, one day, when we return home, and I must believe we will.

I want my son to feel the burnished earth between his toes, wintering in the Kimberley; squint up into a sky too blue. Complain about the heat. Shout. Speak less properly. Breathe the scorching air where I was born. Splash and squeal in the waterholes; see a real crocodile on a riverbank washed up in the wet; feel his pulse race as he runs barefoot through the red mud, back to Everley. Fate's mockery is not lost on me here: that the places I longed so much to escape I now hold dear.

Eddie is presently playing at my feet on the rug by the fire of the farmhouse floor. He's playing with a little tin train, and he's stuffed his baby sister's mittens into the trucks strung behind the engine. 'It's a cloud train, Mummy,' he tells me. It's raining, and his sister, Grace, is asleep in her cradle over the other side of the hearth. This picture is a Christmas-card idyll – all we need is a little snow. Our cottage is spacious and warm, vine-covered; Dad's cousin Joe – Joe Sandstock – has been so generous, letting us rent this place for next to nothing, in exchange for a deal on Sussex milkers with Dad, which has enabled Joe to build himself and his family a much larger house, and one nearer the village of Capel-le-Ferne. Enabled me, too, to learn to cook. Keep house. Appreciate the simple things.

But of course liberty comes with tougher conditions than this.

Airships sail from their cliff-top station here, grey clouds patrolling the coast, and in good weather Eddie and I can hear the guns across the Strait of Dover. Eddie doesn't know what they are, of course, because I tell him it's only thunder. Distant, rolling thunder that holds me inside it sometimes for hours on end. On the bleakest nights, from this vantage, I see it as a smudge of light, throbbing somewhere over the sea.

All is quiet tonight, though, as darkness falls. I listen and listen; it's even stopped raining.

'Come on, Choo-Choo Chumpy Chops, time for bed.' I cuddle Eddie up and we head for the nursery.

'No, Mummy – no!'

'Yes, yes.' I kiss his half-hearted protests; he's almost asleep before we get there.

And once there, as I tuck him in under the blankets, I see the moon rise through the bare branches of the elm that sprawls outside the window, and I kiss him again. I kiss my boy as my mother once kissed me, and each time I do I forgive her a little more. I forgive her the quiet terror, and the even quieter loneliness, that took her from me. My mother, Selena, named for the goddess of the moon. And me, Irene, daughter of Poseidon, daughter of the sea, goddess of peace. Please. I forgive her for being run down by it all, because I understand something of terror and loneliness now, too.

It's November, almost winter, and Fin hates the cold. He hates the cold so much he's promised we'll never go to Glasgow; we haven't yet made it to London, either, except to change trains. But I don't think it's much warmer in Flanders, where he is this night, I must suppose. Somewhere across the water where the world is at war, inside a super cyclone spun from twenty-four-carat greed. And where he is in fact a lieutenant today, for his sins, because one thing Marksy and Old Hal couldn't do between them was convince the Royal Navy to drop the charge of desertion against him. By the time the legal arguments had gone to and fro across the globe, including a lengthy defence from a chap called Rigby, who detailed not only the bona fides of Fin's true decency but the abuses against him, the guns were in place and this was the compromise: rejoin any of the services voluntarily and the past will be allowed to disappear. He chose the Australian expeditionary force, because Australia is where he wants home to be, too. Because it's warm. Because it's not here.

Here, where his swift rise up the ranks has had less to do with his character than …

Rumours say the Battle of Somme has ended, though; that America will join the war soon. I don't know what to believe. Is there any such thing as truth in war? Is there anything to be believed in it? Ocea's last letter, six months old, told me rumours of a battle at Mowla Station, on Geegully Creek south of Derby, with three hundred blacks killed. *War is everywhere*, she wrote, and added, *but here, at least we have the police tell us it never happened.* And in this here? How many are killed? A hundred thousand? A million? Who would know what is happening?

There is nothing for me to believe other than that Fin will survive this. Why shouldn't he? He's survived everything else. He's a professional survivor.

I beg the moon to take him my kiss.

Back in the sitting room I look into the fire for a while; I can't imagine the fire he walks through. His eyes hold only more secrets each time he returns.

And he will return again, possibly at Christmas. We will meet him off the train at Folkestone. He will let Eddie drag him out into the snow to play. He will meet his daughter.

Until then, in the quiet, alone and terrified, I write. I touch the cool of my mother's pearls at my neck and I write: *I am the sea. I am the air. I know all stories …*

Because I want to know them. Because I need to understand.

I write a story about wickedness, and lust; storms unleashed. I write a story about searching souls; about liars, lovers and thieves. I write a story about Fin and me.

AUTHOR NOTE

The story of *Jewel Sea* sprang straight from a sweet piece of serendipity. Idling through Goodreads one rainy afternoon, I chanced upon Annie Boyd's wonderful history, *Koombana Days* – a book I immediately had to order for myself, and one to which I owe a huge debt of gratitude now, not least because Annie has given me kind permission to reproduce her excellent map showing the Nor'-West Run at the front of this book.

I was amazed that I'd never heard of the wreck of the *Koombana* before. The loss of this ship remains one of Australia's worst civilian maritime disasters – indeed Australia's own scaled-down *Titanic* – and one that remains a mystery to this day.

From that amazement I set forth on my own re-imagining of the events, and I must stress the imaginative here. While many of the characters in the story are based on real people who were on the ship when it went down – such as the pearl magnate Abraham Davis, the Skamp sisters, Captain Tom Allen, Hedley Harris, Frank Buttle and Mrs Freer – my portrayal of them, their actions and thoughts, is absolutely fictional. Historical details on them all were far too scarce for me to do much more than merely borrow their names; and I chose to do so more in order that those names be remembered than for any other reason.

The legend of the cursed rose-coloured pearl is also 'real', this pearl having been rumoured at the time to have been brought on board the ship by Abraham Davis. Indeed, the murdered dealer Mark Liebglid, and those convicted of his murder – Charles Hagen, Simeon Espada and Pablo Marquez – were all real people who were implicated in the legend of the curse as well. But while the real-life facts of the disaster and the roseate pearl remain sketchy and contradictory at best, my retelling is only so much more speculation and invention. As Ion Idriess says in his own and very fabulous exploration of the Nor'-West pearling industry, *Forty Fathoms Deep*, 'I am conscious I have only gleaned in a field rich with romance.'

The Indigenous story thread of Warlitj in *Jewel Sea* is fictional too, but was inspired by the real unnamed prisoner recorded as having been on board the *Koombana*, as well as the very real frontier conflicts that continued in the Nor'-West at that time. I have, however, deliberately not named any particular Aboriginal nations of Western Australia, and my inclusion of any spiritual belief has not been taken from any specific tradition or Dreaming story, out of respect for Indigenous ownership of their stories, which, for them, are very much alive today. Warlitj's story is included to acknowledge the realities of the European invasion in Western Australia, and to explore more fully the concepts of law, justice, belief and magic at play throughout my narrative; not to exploit the culture of the peoples who live in the Nor'-West today, and who continue to suffer the consequences of past conflicts, as well as present failures of policy. It's worth noting here that the Mowla conflict mentioned briefly at the end of the novel was in fact a massacre for which I could find no precise date; this says enough in itself of the way history has treated the First Nations people of Western Australia, and across the continent. This says much about my reasons for wanting to include such detail in my own stories, too, however clumsy my attempts might be.

Apologies must go also to John Keats for my plundering of 'Ode on a Grecian Urn' throughout, and to William Blake for pinching and chopping up the first stanza of 'The Tyger' for use as epigraphs, but it is in good part the fault of these poets that I'm such a romantic, in every sense, myself. Just call me a classical sentimentalist.

As always, my debt to the National Library of Australia's Trove is as vast as their collections of newspapers, photographs and ephemera – I could not piece together my pictures of the times without these resources. Fathomless thanks also to Lou Johnson, my publisher, for her faith in the enduring power of stories, and for taking a punt on me. Thanks, too, must go to my editor, Alex Nahlous, for her sharp mind and soulful care of my words. And forever, to my own salty seadog and muse de bloke, Dean Brownlee – none of this happens without your belief in me.

Finally, to all those souls lost on the *Koombana*, I hope in some small way I have helped to keep your story alive. I hope the sea gives up her secret one day to tell us where you rest.

*Take a journey through time with Kim Kelly.
You've never seen Australia like this before …*

LADY BIRD & THE FOX
What happens when a hardworking farm girl and a spoilt rich-boy gambler are mistaken for bushrangers on the road to the goldrush? At a breakneck gallop through wild colonial Australia, *Lady Bird & The Fox* untangles a tale of true love – and true identity.

WILD CHICORY
A journey from Ireland to Australia in the early 1900s, along threads of love, family, war and peace, *Wild Chicory* is a slice of ordinary life rich in history, folklore and fairy tale, and a portrait of the precious bond between a granddaughter, Brigid, and her grandmother, Nell.

PAPER DAISIES
A haunting tale of love, murder and misogyny. Unfolding at the dawn of 1901, as Australia at last becomes a nation and her women rally for the right to vote, *Paper Daisies* tells of the dangerous path one woman must tread to see justice done – and the man who lights her way.

THE BLUE MILE
Against the glittering backdrop of Sydney Harbour, *The Blue Mile* is a story of the cruelties of Great Depression poverty, the wild gamble a city took to build a bridge – a wonder of the world – and the risks only the brave will take for a chance to truly live and love.

THIS RED EARTH
It's 1939 and the girl next door wants adventure before she settles down – but war gives her more than she's asked for. From Australia's sparkling coastline to her dusty, desert heart, *This Red Earth* charts a fight for home, and a quest to tell the truth about love – before it's too late.

BLACK DIAMONDS
From the foothills of the Blue Mountains to the battlefields of France, comes a story of war and coal. Told with freshness, verve and wit, *Black Diamonds* is the tale of a fierce young nation – Australia – and two fierce hearts who dare to discover what courage really means.

For links to all major retailers, please visit: kimkellyauthor.com/books/

KIM KELLY

Kim Kelly is the author of seven novels exploring Australia and its history. Her stories shine a bright light on some forgotten corners of the past and tell the tales of ordinary people living through extraordinary times.

An editor and literary consultant by trade, stories fill her everyday – most nights, too – and it's love that fuels her intellectual engine. In fact, she takes love so seriously she once donated a kidney to her husband to prove it, and also to save his life.

Originally from Sydney, today Kim lives on a small rural property in central New South Wales just outside the tiny gold-rush village of Millthorpe, where the ghosts are mostly friendly and her grown sons regularly come home to graze.